Murder of a Clown

DEXTER JAMES

Murder of a Clown

OTHER BOOKS BY DEXTER JAMES:

Genesis Series:

Genesis Déjà vu – The Beginning

Genesis Déjà vu – The New Eden

Heist During the Rio Games

The Ultimate Conspiracy

Of Ghosts and Aliens

Ghost Marina on the Mississippi

Other Mario Simpson Mysteries:

Murder of a Late-Night TV Host

Murder of a Multitude

Once More, To

My late, wonderful, wife Jean

Contents

Sunday 16th December 2018

Chapter 1

The interior of the Gardens in New York City had been transformed to represent the 'Big Top', hosted by Baxter Family Circus. The circus was in town for four days performing two shows a day. Today's matinee's performance was just about to commence with every seat in the auditorium occupied. The air was full of the smell of cotton candy and popcorn as the excitement was beginning to mount. Suddenly, the main arena lights began to dim and the orchestra opened the matinee's entertainment with the familiar, circus-themed music, the 'Entry of the Gladiators'. A revolving orb high above the center of the circus-ring began to rotate and various colored beams were reflecting sparkling beams of light onto the audience. Spotlights were switched on that were directed at a tunnel that led into the circus-ring. The lights revealed a troupe of performers wearing colorful, sequined costumes parading into the ring. There were clowns, jugglers, acrobats and other players, some of them cartwheeling, others somersaulting but eventually, all of them were waving enthusiastically to the audience. A trio of young men entered the ring, two of them began agilely climbing on the shoulders of one of them, in turn, one of the other men scrambled on top of the other until they were standing perfectly balanced in a three-man tower. With waving arms and a look of horror on their faces, they feigned a fall and then rolled expertly along the floor before jumping up and waving to the packed audience. The majority of the audience were children and their parents had been struggling to contain their offspring's excitement in anticipation of the show; they were now in rapture. Like many modern circuses, this one included no animals in its acts; the entertainment was all performed by humans.

The entertainers made a circle on the perimeter of the circus-ring and began walking around on top of it so that the whole audience received a glimpse of each of the performers. Then the Ringmaster made a regal entrance, to the surprise of many in the audience and the delight of the many dads in attendance, the Ringmaster was a tall, beautiful, buxom blonde wearing the requisite top-hat, a red tailcoat, emblazoned with gold braid and buttons, black leather hot-pants and black knee-high boots that accentuated her long, shapely, legs. Her opening address to the audience revealed a surprisingly deep voice that echoed clearly around the circus.

"Ladies and gentlemen, boys and girls, children of all ages," the Ringmaster began, "welcome to the circus. This afternoon you will witness amazing feats, death-defying acts, and of course the hilarious antics of our clowns." Just at that timely juncture, a clown, one of challenged height, who happened to be carrying a plank of wood, approached the Ringmaster and made an abrupt turn, slapping the

Ringmaster's delightful rear-end with the board as he did so. The clown pretended that he hadn't seen her standing there, he immediately dropped the plank and ran towards the safety of the ring's perimeter, but before he could reach his destination he tripped and fell headfirst into a conveniently placed bucket of water. Now the bucket was stuck on the clown's head and he had to be assisted by other clowns in the troupe. This side-show continued while the Ringmaster completed her introductions.

"As you can see," the Ringmaster continued as though nothing unusual had happened and pointed to the huge cannon positioned near the entrance of the circus-ring, "our first act will be to shoot a man from a cannon. Now, children, there will be a loud bang accompanied by fireworks then a man will be fired from this cannon, all the way to that net over there." The Ringmaster explained as she theatrically moved her pointed finger from the cannon to the safety net. "This is an extremely dangerous act but there is one man who dares to carry out this perilous performance and it is," the Ringmaster's voice now rose to announce the daredevil, accompanied by a drum-roll for a more dramatic effect, "'The Great Grando' the Human Cannonball." The Ringmaster stepped back as the searchlights shone on a man dressed in a tight, white sequined, one-piece suit exiting the tunnel. He approached the front of the cannon, his name, 'The Great Grando,' was emblazoned in red on the back of his tunic and the whole ensemble was topped off with a red crash-helmet and black visor. He raised his arm to acknowledge the crowd while the other performers returned through the tunnel as the orchestra reprised the circus theme music.

By the time the Great Grando reached the center of the arena all the other performers had left, and the attention of the entire audience was firmly on the Human Cannonball as he began walking towards the cannon. The cannon itself was fixed onto a rig that was used to transport the gun from venue to venue. Naturally, the vehicle itself was concealed by drapes, bunting and placards depicting artistic representations of the Great Grando. The Great Grando began to climb onto the rig with the use of a drop-down ladder fixed underneath the muzzle of the cannon. Once on top of the rig, he gave another wave to the audience ensuring he circled so that everyone obtained a good view of the daredevil. He then stepped onto a curved-top box that doubled as a housing to secure the cannon during travel and also as a step during the act. This gave him enough height so that he could reach two handles situated on top of the cannon. He grabbed the handles and theatrically lifted his legs, like a gymnast, and placed them into the bore of the cannon. After entering the cannon, he released his grip on the handles and twisted his body so that he was now lying face down. There he paused to wave once more to the audience. By now, all the other performers had retired through the tunnel, the orchestra had stopped playing their music, the audience's attention was firmly fixed on the Great Grando. The Great Grando gave a final wave to the audience before disappearing down the bore of the cannon and a solitary drummer began to play an anticipatory drum roll.

The Ringmaster began to chant a countdown and by the time she had called out 'eight', the audience, began shouting out the numbers with her, right on cue. As the Ringmaster shouted out 'five', the drummer began beating harder, the audience was shouting out the numbers louder and the noise was reaching a crescendo. The house lights began to dim and by the time the Ringmaster shouted 'one', the whole circus became pitch black. Suddenly, there was a flash of light, followed by a loud boom emitting from the cannon. Next, fireworks were being ignited followed by a series of bangs even louder than the first one. The arena's lights came back on, but the audience did not see the Great Grando being flung across the length of the circus-ring. What they did witness, to the horror of them all, was a lifeless, human fireball that was barely emitted from the mouth of the cannon. Fire swiftly began to envelop both the cannon and also the body of what was once the Great Grando as it fell unceremoniously into the inferno that was now erupting all around the vehicle.

Sunday 16th December 2018

Chapter 2

It was obvious to everyone, that something had gone terribly wrong, well almost everyone. There were always those cynics who thought that this was all part of the act, but as the house lights came back on, many of the performers could be seen rushing to the scene with water-hoses, buckets of water and fire-extinguishers; now even the nay-sayers were swayed. Similar to performers on cruise-ships, circus performers double as emergency personnel and assistants during the setting up and taking down of the circus tent, sometimes, even as extra clowns. Whenever the cannon is fired, many of the performers are on hand in the event of a situation such as the one now unfolding in the circus-ring. The current problem was that not only were fireworks continuing to randomly ignite but the heat radiating from the incandescent fire was preventing the performers from getting close to the flames and all they could do was try and contain the fire and not let it progress beyond the circus-ring.

Audience members who were seated within close proximity of the inferno were forced to flee their seats and take shelter in the upper seating areas, not only because of the intense heat but also because of the toxic smells emanating from the fire. The acrid odor was a combination of spent fireworks, explosives, the burning of rubber, wood, material, oil and not least of all, human flesh.

The Ringmaster had known that the performance had gone badly awry and had immediately contacted 911 using her cell phone. Pending the emergency teams' arrival, she organized a clear route through the tunnel so that easy and rapid access could be obtained. Her quick thinking was opportune as the fire department arrived within minutes. It took the fireman over an hour to contain the fire and ensure that all the embers had been finally extinguished.

Once the Ringmaster had contacted the emergency services, she instructed the Garden's staff to evacuate the building. Fortunately, there was no panic, and everyone left in an orderly fashion. The debacle had left the performers in a state of shock. It was always difficult when they lost one of their own, there was such camaraderie amongst the performers. Needless to say, the remainder of the afternoon's performance was canceled, as was the one scheduled for that evening. There was even doubt that the rest of the week's performances would continue as scheduled. Eventually, most of the performers returned to their respective trailers to mourn the loss of their fallen comrade, others hung around the circus arena consoling each other. All that was left to do was for the emergency teams to sift through the burnt-out remains of the cannon in search of the charred body of the unfortunate Great Grando.

Monday 17th December 2018

Chapter 3

Detective Darlene Knight was seated on the corner of her skipper's desk, Detective Pete Cannatelli, explaining the tragedy that had occurred during her visit to the circus the previous day. Darlene was dressed in her usual office clothes consisting of running shoes, tight blue jeans, and an NYPD jacket over a white blouse. Her long blonde hair was, as usual, tied up above her collar, as per regulations. Pete Cannatelli had recently been promoted to a supervisory position, something that he had always shunned, until now. His family was growing, the extra money would come in handy, and now that his boss had been promoted he knew that if he turned this opportunity down he would either be transferred to another department or some go-getter, still wet behind the ears, would be parachuted in above him. Neither option would have been acceptable.

Pete was also dressed in jeans, but he certainly didn't look as good in his as Darlene did in hers. To complete his ensemble, he also wore a faded, Led Zeppelin t-shirt, his usual scruffy sneakers and a black NYPD hoody. His long brown hair and the stubble on his chin merely added to his scruffy appearance. Pete had been looking at the photo of the fire in the newspaper when Darlene had entered the office and brought him over a coffee and a donut.

"Did you and Humph witness this?" Pete asked, referring to Humph, the Chief Medical Officer, while he pointed to the photograph in the newspaper. Humph had received the complimentary tickets for the circus during the team's previous case.

"Sure did, it was horrifying!" Darlene replied.

"I bet it was," Pete agreed. "Were your seats close to the fire?" Pete asked.

"No, we were seated kind of kitty-corner to the cannon," Darlene explained, "we would have had a wonderful view of the Great Grando hurtling through the air and landing in the net but of course all we saw was the explosion and the fire."

"Firing a man from a cannon is a dangerous act. Some thirty human cannonballs have been killed over the years, but normally it's the landing that goes wrong, not the cannon itself blowing up."

"How do you know this shit Pete?" Darlene asked. Pete was full of useless information which always dumbfounded Darlene as to where he got his knowledge.

"Grew up loving circuses and vaudeville acts, especially the illusionists, Houdini and the like. I used to read up on it, trying to figure out how the tricks were done. Most of them are amazingly simple when you know how," Pete replied, "by the way, where is Humph?" Because Humph was voluntarily suspended from driving, due to a broken ankle, another throwback to their last case together,

Darlene was temporarily acting as his chauffeur and staying at his place to help him out with the daily chores.

“I left him at the front desk,” Darlene explained, “Larry is on duty this morning so Humph was giving him a first-hand account of the scene.”

Larry was a long-time cop who was now designated to desk duty; he was the first policeman Humph had met on his first day in the department.

“You know, I don’t think you should attend any more functions at the Gardens,” Pete mentioned casually.

“Why’s that?” Darlene asked with a questioning look on her face.

“Well that’s two events you’ve been to and both of them have ended up with the audience being evacuated,” Pete replied with a laugh, referring to their last case.

“True!” Darlene replied simply.

As Darlene and Pete were talking, a staccato sound could be heard getting louder as it came closer. Then, through the doors came Humph, his walking stick hitting the wooden floor as he limped into the office. His broken ankle was healing well, but he would be forced to use the cane for a few more days although it didn’t stop him from maintaining his penchant for sharp clothes. Humph, was a bespectacled, short, and to be polite, a plump man with a clean-shaven face topped with thin, wispy hair. He removed his coat and hung it up on the coat rack behind his temporary desk. His main office was in the morgue but since the accident and because of his growing attachment to Darlene he spent most of his rehabilitation time in the precinct building. Today, Humph was dressed in a tailored blue pin-striped, 3-piece suit with the mandatory outrageous tie. As Humph began to walk towards the others Pete could see that today's choice of tie depicted a bi-plane on top of a bright red background.

"Good morning all," Humph said jovially.

"Morning Humph, so what's with the tie?" Pete asked.

"Ah that, well, it is to celebrate the Wright Brothers' historic first flight on this day in 1903," Humph replied.

"You know that's not strictly true," Pete began, "it has been officially recognized by Jane's, that's the leading aviation journal, that a German pilot, one Gustav Weisskopf, made a successful flight some two years before the Wright Brothers."

"How do you know this shit Pete?" Humph asked belligerently, then seeing the picture of the fiery cannon in the newspaper he forgot about his tie, "anyway, I see you have found out what occurred during our exciting trip to the circus yesterday," Humph said to Pete while Darlene handed him a coffee.

"What, no donut?" Humph asked disdainfully as he looked cravingly at the one Pete was eating.

"Not for you young man, you're on a diet, remember?" Darlene said as she tapped Humph's pronounced belly.

"Yes, I heard it was quite an outing for you both," Pete said.

"Poor guy, I wonder what went wrong," Humph said as he took a sip of his coffee.

"Pyrotechnics are fickle," Pete began, "especially if it's a chain reaction, one errant spark and it could all go wrong very quickly. Talk of the devil, here's a man who would know more about that than I do."

Chuck Gorman from the Bomb Disposal Unit had just walked into the office. Chuck was a big burly, ex-military man who still maintained a buzz-cut almost like a medal but today he was looking very tired and a little bedraggled. His uniform was covered in dirt and black smudges covered his handsome face and strong hands. Darlene handed him a coffee.

"Here, I think you need this more than I do," Darlene said.

"Cheers, I've been down at the circus all night sifting through the remnants of that fire," Chuck said, pointing to the picture in the newspaper on Pete's desk. Then he asked, "where's Mario?"

"Ah, so that explains your appearance," Pete replied, "as for Mario, our illustrious leader is in Miami with that well-known superstar, Magill."

After the team's last case their Chief of Detectives, Eugene Horowitz, had decided to retire and Mario Simpson was promoted to the Chief's position. Mario had become the youngest detective in the NYPD to attain that position. The case had involved Magill, a world-famous singer from England and during the investigation, Mario had struck up a romantic relationship with her. He was currently visiting her in Miami, her last concert date before returning to England for the Christmas break.

"When are you expecting him back?" Chuck asked, looking a little pensive.

"Not sure, yet; he may be traveling with Magill back to England for the Christmas holidays," Pete replied. He had known Chuck for a long time, they had worked together on many cases and he was sensing there was something amiss. "Anything I can help you with buddy?"

"Well, it concerns the death of 'The Great Grando'," Chuck answered, once more cocking his head towards the picture in the newspaper. "I've been working with the fire department investigating the combustion materials that caused the fire and the fireworks that were used during the act."

"And what have you found out?" Pete asked as he was about to take a sip of his coffee, but Chuck's reply halted his action before the cup met his lips and it also sent chills around the room.

“Well, from what we have uncovered to date, I can tell you it was no accident.”

Monday 17th December 2018

Chapter 4

"What?" Darlene and Humph both said at the same time. Then Humph added, "we were there at the performance. We saw it first-hand."

"Well, your eye-witness reports may be useful in establishing how and why 'The Great Grando' was killed," Chuck replied. Darlene and Humph were left looking at each other with their jaws agape. Pete had a more pragmatic attitude towards the revelation.

"So, what makes you think it wasn't just an accident, Chuck," Pete asked, before making another attempt to drink his coffee.

"Well, it wasn't just pyrotechnics that caused that fire. There were also high explosive incendiaries strategically placed in and around the front of the cannon. It was substantially more than just fireworks. Those circus performers did a terrific job of preventing the whole arena from being burnt down before the fire department showed up," Chuck replied.

"Wow, to think we could have been killed," Darlene whispered.

"How did it get detonated?" Pete asked.

"Haven't got the answer to that one," Chuck replied despondently, "what's more we may never know. Any evidence has been almost obliterated by the fire and the firemen who were fighting the flames.

Not their fault I might add, it's a bitch trying to extinguish incendiaries."

"But who would want to do such a thing?" Humph asked.

"Just as importantly, how did the person who set those explosives come by such sophisticated munitions?" Chuck said, rhetorically, "they're not the sort of thing you can pick up on any street corner and it would have been no easy feat to set them up in that congested space under the cannon."

"So, I don't understand," Pete began, "why are you here? Why do you want to speak with Mario? I have had more experience in these types of cases than he has."

"Oh, for sure you have," Chuck replied, "that's precisely why I suggested to the Fire Chief that he should recommend to the Commissioner that your team is assigned to the case. Now that Mario is the man, I just wanted to call in on my way home to give him a heads-up that's all. Because even as we speak, the Fire Chief is going through the appropriate channels to officially assign the case to this team."

Monday 17th December 2018

Chapter 5

"Assigned to this team?" Pete asked incredulously, "why?"

"Well, you're homicide, aren't you? And as far as I'm concerned, it's a potential murder investigation. Why not assign it to you?" Chuck replied, arms outstretched in a 'what's the problem' attitude.

"If as you say there were heavy-duty incendiary explosives used, what was left of the body, Chuck?" Humph asked.

"Ha, to be honest," Chuck responded, "hardly anything. The emergency services were trampling all over the scene in their attempts to extinguish the fire. As I mentioned, incendiaries are tough to put out. So good luck with that one."

"What difference would the incendiaries make Humph?" Darlene asked.

"Well, a human body doesn't turn completely to ash upon burning, the skeleton will still survive," Humph answered.

"But when someone is cremated, doesn't the body turn to ash?" Darlene wondered.

"No, the skeletal remains are taken from the cremator and the remains placed into a machine known as a cremulator, which grinds the bones into ash," Humph explained.

"So, is it possible you could still get DNA from the remains?" Pete asked.

"DNA identification becomes very difficult to obtain after severe burning and is inaccurate at best. It is unlikely that we could get a positive id. from the body," Humph explained, "even dental record identification could be a problem. The only thing we could ascertain with any certainty is the victim's approximate age-at-death and sex," Humph told them.

"I wonder if the person who set up the explosives knew that!" Pete said with his usual cynicism.

"Well, I think what you will be confirming is that it is the body of 'The Great Grando'. According to the Ringmaster, everyone else is accounted for, only 'The Great Grando' is AWOL," Chuck said. "The Fire Chief asked her to carry out a roll call to confirm no one else was missing and all indications are that there was only the one body caught up in the inferno."

"Asked ***her***?" Pete said in a surprised tone.

"Yes, Pete, the Ringmaster is a woman!" Darlene cajoled him.

"A good-looking one at that," Chuck smiled lasciviously at Pete, "look, just a thought, but I'm not the detective here, I think whoever did this figured that everyone was just going to put this down to a performance that went horribly wrong and that a serious investigation would not be necessary. Even then, there's going to be little or no evidence left to tell the tale. Death will probably be considered as an open verdict."

"So, you're leaning towards murder?" Pete asked.

"Either murder or suicide. You see, there is no place for those types of incendiary explosives to be used in any situation in civilian life, especially in a circus," Chuck replied.

"Suicide?" Darlene asked, "I would have thought burning yourself to death would be a horrible way to die. Are you sure?"

"It's likely the victim wouldn't have known anything about it. In the confined space of that cannon, the initial blast of the explosives would have rendered anyone in there unconscious and those incendiaries would have burned through human flesh in seconds," Chuck explained before completely changing his demeanor. "Look, it's been a slice chatting with you, but I'm beat, I just wanted to stop by and give you the good news. Meanwhile, I have to go home, clean up, and get some sleep. I'll check in with you during the next couple of days when I have a little more information to give to you. Thanks for the coffee, Darlene." He took a final swig of his coffee and used the empty cup to toast Darlene in thanks.

"No problem Chuck," Darlene replied.

For the next hour or so the three of them discussed the previous day's events with Pete asking various questions to obtain a feel for the scene. Their conversation was interrupted by a phone call. It was Commissioner Harper.

Monday 17th December 2018

Chapter 6

"Good morning detective, Commissioner Harper here," the perfect media voice with the Hamptons accent boomed over the phone lines.

"Good morning Commissioner," Pete replied calmly as he looked up at Darlene then across to Humph, who immediately stopped talking. "What can I do for you," knowing perfectly well what was coming.

"Yes, well, I'm sure you have heard about this tragic accident that occurred at the Gardens yesterday," the Commissioner replied. "I was discussing the case with the Fire Chief and we need to send a team over to investigate right away, but I'm sure it will turn out to be nothing more than the accident it appears to be. My goodness, we couldn't have another incident in such a short space of time at the Gardens, now could we? It would be bad for tourism." The Commissioner was referring to the team's last investigation regarding a serial killer that culminated in the capture of the perpetrator at the Gardens.

"No sir, that we can't," Pete merely agreed.

"As soon as the Fire Chief called me, I immediately knew which team I wanted to assign this case to. So, I am officially assigning the case to my top, intrepid team of detectives, I'd like to get this wrapped up as soon as possible, preferably before the holidays. Good day," the Commissioner said before abruptly hanging up.

"Well, it's official, we're on the case," Pete told the others.

After lunch, the three of them drove down to the Gardens to begin their investigation into the death of the Great Grando. As they approached the arena Darlene held open a door for Humph just as one of the circus clowns happened to be exiting. The clown was laughing as he limped by pointing at Humph's cane. The detectives didn't quite know what to make of that. Was he making fun of Humph or commiserating as he continued to limp as he walked away?

"That was a funny ***gesture***!" Pete said, attempting a play on words with ***jester*** but, it fell on deaf ears.

When they walked into the arena the site of the fire had been cordoned off with yellow police tape. There were three people in white protective suits together with a couple of fire-fighters stepping delicately through the rubble within the confines of the tape. Around the outside perimeter of the tape, a few of the circus performers were milling around, curious as to what the white-suited people were looking for. As Pete approached the scene, one of the members of the group from inside the taped perimeter saw him and came over to greet him.

“So, the hot team has been assigned this one then, have they? Where’s pretty boy?” Harry said as she removed her head-covering to reveal a vast mop of wiry, curly red hair. Harry was short for Harriet and she was a no-nonsense investigator in charge of the forensics team assigned to the case. Standing at only five-feet-tall, she was a diminutive lady, but at 45 years old, with five children and being married to a cop, she’d seen it all, done it all, and took no crap from anyone. She also just happened to get on very well with Pete and the absent Mario, having worked with them on numerous previous cases.

“Mario is taking a few days vacation, visiting with Magill,” Pete replied, “so you’re stuck with me.”

“Ah, could be worse,” Harry said and then turning to the others, “hey Darlene, hi Humph. Not sure what data you’re going to get from this lot, it’s a mess.” Harry said.

Darlene had noticed that the other two white-suited individuals were Harry’s assistants and crime scene photographers. Darlene had the misfortune to have encountered them during previous cases, although she had not been formally introduced to either of them and had no wish to. One of them noticed her and quickly snapped off a couple of photos of Darlene, much to her chagrin.

“Have you managed to locate any pieces of the body?” Humph asked.

"Bits, but it is so intertwined with the wreckage of the cannon and much of it has been trod on by the firefighters. Not their fault of course," Harry explained, confirming what Chuck had already told them.

"Well, whatever you find that you think is relevant could you have it sent to the lab. please. I should get there at some point during the next day or two," Humph replied.

"Takes more than a broken foot to stop you Humph!" Harry laughed.

At that moment, the Ringmaster approached them and introduced herself.

"Hi, pleased to meet you, I'm Gwendoline Baxter, Ringmaster, at your service. Are you the detectives I was told would be arriving to investigate the accident?" Gwendoline asked, instantly charming Pete.

"Yes, we are, I'm Detective Cannatelli," Pete replied as he introduced the rest of the team. Gwendoline shook hands with each of the three of them, while Pete noted that Chuck had not been wrong about Gwendoline; she was a looker alright. Tall, courtesy of her beautiful long legs, perfect for a female Ringmaster. She was dressed casually in tight jeans that accentuated her hourglass figure and a red t-shirt that was struggling to contain her large breasts. The t-shirt was custom-made with the name of the circus, 'Baxter Family Circus', printed on the back with a picture of a circus tent on the front. Over her left breast was her initials 'GB'. Her long blond hair was fixed upon her head with wisps stranding down across her rosy cheeks. If all that was not enough, she had the bluest eyes Pete had ever seen.

"This is a sad day for all of us. The Great Grando got on with everyone, we're all shocked by this accident," Gwendoline said. "Look, I hate to be a pain, but I'm not just the Ringmaster I also happen to be the owner of this circus and I know you're going to have a lot of questions for me but I've decided to cancel the rest of the performances here in New York. Needless to say, there's so much I have to take care of, so for now, can I just introduce you to someone for your immediate questions and I promise I will be available to you tomorrow? Is that acceptable?"

"Sure," Pete said submissively, Darlene merely smiled. Pete would put Gwendoline's age at somewhere in her late twenties, very young to own a circus, he thought. Humph saw the members of the fire department picking over the debris with the forensics team so he was about to take his leave to survey what was left of the cannon but was held back by Gwendoline.

"Anton! Anton!" Gwendoline shouted, and a young man began walking towards them. "This is Anton, he has worked as Petr's assistant for the past few years. He should be able to answer many of your questions."

"Petr?" Pete asked.

“Oh sorry, the Great Grando, his real name was Petr Stojanovski. I believe he originally came from Macedonia. O.K., I’ll leave you in Anton’s capable hands and I will catch you later,” Gwendoline said. She then began to walk away, barking out orders to people as she did so.

Anton was a tall, shy-looking, young, man who looked like one of those proverbial kids who ran away to join the circus. His tousled dark hair and pale complexion gave him a forlorn look, giving Pete the impression that he could be a bit of a loner. Although, the kid was fit-looking with hardly an ounce of body fat on him.

“Anton, I’m Detective Cannatelli and this is Detective Knight,” Pete said, “what’s your role in the circus?”

“Hi, I am Petr’s assistant and one day I hope to be the human cannonball,” Anton replied with a smile and a heavy eastern European accent. “Anton Depopoulis at your service.”

“Anton, we are investigating the accident that took place here yesterday,” Pete said.

“I think we all know it was not an accident,” Anton replied.

Monday 17th December 2018

Chapter 7

"Why do you say that, Anton?" Pete asked, surprised at Anton's reaction.

"Petr was, how do you say, matic, metic," Anton began to say as though he was struggling for the right word.

"Do you mean meticulous?" Darlene gently coaxed him.

"Yes, meticulous, that's the word" Anton agreed, nodding his head. "Petr would check, re-check, and check everything again. There was never an error," Anton said with some pride. "I think he deliberately did this to himself, he sabotaged those explosives, he brought about his own death! Otherwise, how could it have happened?"

"Did you assist Petr with the pyrotechnics Anton?" Darlene asked gently.

"No, nobody ever did," Anton replied, "Petr insisted on being solely responsible for the fireworks and the cannon. I helped carry the equipment, but immediately before any performance, it was all Petr. He would wire up all the fireworks so that they would go off in a set sequence. Then, he would concentrate on calculating the figures for the firing of the canon. He would input parameters into an algorithm that he had on his computer and only he knew how they were calculated. What I do know is that it includes factors like the trajectory of the cannon, the torque of the spring that propelled him, distance to the net, and his weight. His weight hardly varied, he was a fitness nut, exercised regularly and always ate healthily, never drank nor smoked. I was hoping to take over from him one day so he would share bits of information with me and he promised to teach me everything. One of those things was a fitness regime that I had been following, we would work out together. Our program consisted of calisthenics, cardio, weights, yoga and pilates exercises, improvising with the equipment we found around the circus." Darlene was thinking that was something she should be doing now that she was staying at Humph's place. It had been a few weeks since she last visited the gym, but for now, she had to put that on the backburner as she continued to listen to Anton. "He promised to let me make an attempt in the cannon one day if I could prove I wasn't going to screw anything up."

"And have you screwed anything up Anton?" Darlene asked with a smile.

"No, not once," Anton replied, both passionately and proudly.

"What was Petr's schedule before a performance?" Pete asked.

"We would set up the fireworks and the explosives –" Anton began but was interrupted by Darlene.

"You said 'we', I thought you said earlier it was just Petr who dealt with the fireworks?" Darlene asked.

"That's right, but part of my job was to transport them on a trolley from the safe to the cannon. It's a fireproof safe that we always keep in a secure area away from the circus-ring," Anton explained.

"How much explosive was necessary for the cannon?" Pete asked

"Actually, none," Anton replied, "the cannon is purely spring-loaded. The explosives are just for effect." Pete nodded his head in understanding, he already knew that, but he wanted to hear Anton's response. He indicated to Anton to continue. "After the cannon was ready, Petr would return to the trailer and weigh himself; then he would make his calculations. Once that was done, he would prepare for the performance. After he was fully dressed in his tunic and helmet, he would weigh himself again immediately before the performance. He would run his calculations again and if necessary, he would make the slightest of adjustments to the angle of the cannon or the tension of the spring. Petr left no room for error." Anton began to get a little emotional and a solitary tear appeared running down his cheek, but his face turned to a mask of despair. "The number of fireworks and explosives that exploded yesterday was far more than I took from the safe. Petr must at some point, when I wasn't around, obtained more explosives from the safe and deliberately tampered with the pyrotechnics. He must have altered the setting of the spring because for all his performances, once he had completed his adjustments, those explosives and fireworks always ignited on time and once the cannon was fired, he would always hit the center of the net."

Monday 17th December 2018

Chapter 8

"Would anyone else have access to this area after Petr and you had completed the setup?" Pete asked. His hands were in his pockets and he was trying to be relaxed in an attempt to placate Anton.

"No, nobody," Anton replied hunching his shoulders. "We were the only people allowed in this area; it was restricted!"

"So, let me understand this correctly," Pete began. "You and Petr are the only people who had access to the cannon and nobody else was allowed near it. Is that correct?"

"Yes, that's correct," Anton replied.

"Could it have been a bad batch of explosives or fireworks that spoilt the sequence?" Pete asked.

"No, there were far too many explosives used yesterday. Petr wouldn't have made that mistake," Anton replied adamantly. Pete thought about that for a while before replying.

"I just want to clarify, if you were the one bringing the fireworks and explosives from the safe you are certain that the correct amount was being used, is that right?" Pete asked.

"Correct, I brought over enough fireworks for one performance, no more," Anton replied vehemently.

“So when do you think the extra explosives got there?” Pete persisted.

“We did our setup at around 10:00, it took around thirty minutes. Petr also had access to the safe, so he could have added more at any time after that initial setup,” Anton suggested. “All I know is that I never saw all those explosives.”

“So you didn’t stay with him after you set up the fireworks?” Pete asked.

“No, I returned to my trailer I share with one of the trapeze artists. Only the big stars have their own trailers,” Anton explained, “Petr would return to his trailer to prepare for the show. He could have added the explosives then.”

“When exactly did you think Petr was going to share with you the secrets of the cannon?” Pete asked, attempting to change the subject a little.

“He promised me that after these performances at the Gardens we would practice during the off-season, down in Florida,” Anton replied proudly. “He has been giving me hints and insights to the working of the cannon.”

“Just one more thing Anton,” Pete began, “had you noticed anything different about Petr during the last few days or weeks? Had he been drinking, was he depressed?”

"As I said earlier, Petr never drank," Anton replied, then his brow creased a little as he appeared to be thinking back. "But, now that you mention it, his mood had changed a little since we arrived in New York."

"In what way Anton?" Darlene asked.

"Quiet, not his usual self," Anton said. "He was usually happy, telling jokes, especially when he was setting up the fireworks. He would joke that one day he would blow himself up if he wasn't careful. And now he has!" Anton's body suddenly convulsed in another round of sobs as Darlene put an arm around his shoulder to console the poor man.

"So, you think it was suicide, do you?" Pete asked gently. Anton merely nodded his head between sobs.

"Yes, but why?" Anton asked, his arms open in a pleading way as if Pete and Darlene knew the answer.

"Suicide would certainly explain everything," Pete said gently. "Maybe you can direct us to his trailer," Pete said, immediately changing the subject.

"Sure, this way," Anton said, and they began walking out to where all the performers' trailers were parked. When they arrived at Petr's trailer Anton went off in search of Gwendoline to obtain a key to the trailer door.

After about a five-minute wait, Anton returned holding up a key and he proceeded to unlock the trailer door. Anton was about to enter the trailer, but Pete held him back.

"Sorry Anton, this is now a crime scene, police only," Pete told the grief-stricken boy. Pete thought he was going to get some hassle, but Anton merely backed off and allowed Pete and Darlene to enter the trailer. Darlene shut the door and in doing so it obliterated most of the light inside the trailer. She searched for a light switch and located one near the door. As she flicked the switch a light that was recessed in the ceiling came on. Three lights ran down the middle of the trailer with one of them shining down on a small writing desk. In the middle of the desk, propped up against a black, plastic pen and pencil organizer was an envelope. The envelope was addressed to, 'To who it may concern'.

Monday 17th December 2018

Chapter 9

Darlene and Pete looked at each other before Pete took out his phone and snapped a couple of pictures of the envelope and the desk.

"Technically, I think it should read, 'to whom it may concern'," Pete said returning his gaze to the envelope.

"Well, if it was Petr, his English may not be good enough to know the subtleties of the English language like you, I certainly wouldn't," Darlene replied. "Should we open it?" Not knowing quite sure what the protocol for this would be, believing it was something Harry's team should be doing first. But Pete took charge.

"Damn right we're going to open it," Pete said immediately. Pete got on his knees to scrutinize the envelope to ensure that it wasn't attached to anything.

"What are you doing Pete?" Darlene asked.

"I want to make sure it's not booby-trapped," Pete replied, "I can't possibly think why it would be but I'm not taking any chances." Darlene stood back as she watched Pete painstakingly look at the envelope from all angles. He then gingerly felt the packet and determined it was far too thin to contain anything other than a letter. Tentatively, he picked up the envelope and held it up to the light. All he could see inside the envelope was what appeared to be a single sheet of paper. At the same time, he was reaching in his pocket for a penknife to use as a letter opener. He pulled out a blade from his penknife and carefully opened the letter. Inside was, as he suspected, a suicide note, handwritten using a biro pen. The handwriting was neat but looked as though it had been written hastily, although the wording was well written, it read:

To Who it may concern,

I have come to that age in my life where I have no real reason to continue and I'm getting far too old to be flung from a cannon two times a day. I visited my bank yesterday, withdrew all my cash, and as I have no dependents, I have given everything to charity.

I apologize for the inconvenience, but the cannon was my life and I decided that was the way I wanted to go. I trust nobody was injured.

My apologies to Anton, I know he was so looking forward to becoming a human cannonball and he still may.

Gwendoline, thank you for all that you and your family have done for me over the years and sorry.

Pete handed the letter to Darlene, she read it quickly.

"You nailed it, skipper," Darlene said, using her new term for Pete now that he had been promoted but Pete ignored the compliment.

"Bag that envelope and the note and let Harriet check it out for prints. Let's give the place a thorough search, see what else we can come up with," Pete said.

Besides the note, they found Petr's wallet and passport. Darlene looked inside the wallet, it contained a few small banknotes, a driver's license, and a few other personal documents. They spent the next two hours searching through the trailer for any piece of evidence that could throw some light on the case. They located bank statements and receipts that verified the withdrawal of funds from the account. In the wardrobe, there were a few clothes, a couple of spare 'Great Grando' tunics together with some clown uniforms, which Darlene thought strange and something she thought they should ask about. They searched the whole trailer, looking in all nooks and crannies, under mattresses, for any false panels or loose floorboards but nothing of any interest was found.

"O.K., I think we're done here," Pete finally said, and they left the trailer, locking the door behind them. They went back into the arena and Pete saw Gwendoline discussing something with one of the crew.

They stood back a few paces while she finished her discussion and then Pete held up the key.

“Petr’s trailer key, thank you,” Pete said.

“Oh, yes, thanks,” Gwendoline said as she accepted the key from Pete. “Any luck with your investigation?”

“I noticed a couple of clown uniforms in Petr’s wardrobe. Did he use those sometimes in his act?” Darlene asked.

“No, he was always the ‘Great Grando’, but like all of us in the circus, sometimes we have to double up doing other things, myself included. On those occasions, Petr became Popo the clown. In fact, he was very good at it,” Gwendoline replied with a cheery look on her face. “I had often told him that if he wanted to hand over the reins to Anton to become the human cannonball, I would gladly hire him as a clown.”

“Had he discussed with you any thoughts of retiring? Maybe because of his age?” Pete asked.

“Not at all, I think he had a few good years left in him, he was still fit,” Gwendoline explained. “After all, the Zacchini brothers were still being fired from a cannon well into their sixties, Petr was only in his forties. He had years left as long as he stayed healthy.”

“Had you noticed any difference in his mood or demeanor during the last little while?” Pete asked.

"No none," Gwendoline replied, looking quizzically at Pete and his line of questioning - until the penny dropped. "Wait a minute! You're not suspecting suicide, are you?"

"Right now, we're not ruling out anything," Pete replied with his poker face. "But thanks, for now, we'll probably have a load more questions for you tomorrow. What time will be good for you?" Pete asked.

"Any time after ten would be good, hopefully, it won't be as hectic as today has been," Gwendoline replied.

As Darlene and Pete left the arena and walked towards their car Darlene appeared a little puzzled.

"Why didn't you tell Gwendoline about Petr's suicide note?" Darlene asked.

"It's all a little too convenient," Pete replied.

"What do you mean? You said yourself, suicide would fit," Darlene replied.

"A few things are pointing me in a different direction," Pete replied.

"Like what?" Darlene asked.

"Overcoat. There was no overcoat hanging in the wardrobe. It's winter and there was no heavy winter clothing in his trailer," Pete explained.

"Is having no overcoat grounds to dismiss this as a suicide?" Darlene asked. "His suitcase, wallet and passport were all there," Darlene offered.

"But not his overcoat," Pete said again. "More significantly, nor was there any sign of a computer or a file for figuring out the algorithm for the cannon. Anton told us he always went to his trailer to figure that all out. Well, where are his figures?"

Tuesday 18th December 2018

Chapter 10

The following morning, Pete was approaching his office area at just before 7:00 AM and he was surprised to see Mario in his office going through the inbox that was heavily laden with a variety of incoming mail.

"Hey man! What are you doing here?" Pete asked with a surprised look. "You're not due back yet, what's up?"

"I'll tell you in a bit. I didn't realize the Chief had to deal with so much crap, look at all this stuff! Most of it is bullshit!" Mario said, riffling through all the papers in the inbox.

"Welcome to senior police work buddy!" Pete smiled. "Have you got to the latest case we're working on yet? Compliments of Commissioner Harper."

"Yeah, I've scanned briefly through the emails, I saw that," Mario replied. "What have you got so far?"

"A couple of avenues we're working on, but Darlene and I are heading down there in a couple of hours. We didn't get to meet with the Ringmaster yesterday, well, at least not to discuss the case. She was up to her ears with problems. She promised to sit down with us today, maybe you'd like to come along, if you can tear yourself away from your desk that is," Pete said sarcastically.

“Very funny, yeah, I’ll tag along,” Mario replied but he was still sifting through his pile of memos.

“Great, I’ll update you on the way, meanwhile, I’ll just leave you to clean up your crap,” Pete replied waving a hand at his paperwork.

“Gee, thanks,” Mario responded. “By the way, did I hear you right, did you say she?”

“Oh, she’s a she alright,” Pete replied ribaldly as he turned to leave.

“Can you shut the door on your way out?” Mario asked. “I don’t want to be disturbed until I’ve cleared this lot up,” Mario once more fanned through the sheath of paperwork in his inbox.

“Oh, excuse me Mr. Bigshot!” Pete said and he did indeed shut the door as he continued walking towards his own desk.

Mario sat at his desk wondering what he had gotten himself into with this promotion. He was a handsome man, dark complexion, dark eyes topped with an unruly mop of dark, curly hair, courtesy of his Italian mother. But it belied a sharp mind and an inquisitive nature, courtesy of his English father, a retired fraud investigator at a major bank. These logic genes from his father had assisted him in becoming a lead detective at the young age of 33 under the tutelage of the recently retired, Chief Horowitz.

Mario knew he would quickly be brought up to speed with the current case, but that didn’t concern him. What was bothering him was the enormity of the task at hand. There was a mountain of memos to attend to, a whole slew of voicemails that required listening to and finally, the bane of the modern era, emails, hundreds of them. As he often did when things began to overwhelm him, he called his dad.

“Simpson here,” came the succinct reply.

“Hi dad, Mario here,” Mario replied as if his dad wouldn’t recognize his son’s voice.

“Mario, how are you doing? Your mother is desperate to know what your plans are for the holidays, Manchester or New York?” Mr. Simpson asked. He and his wife were aware of his trip with Magill but where Mario would be for Christmas was still very much in the air.

“I‘m back in New York, back at work, so I will be home for the holidays. Probably arrive at the house Christmas Eve,” Mario replied.

“Oh, I’m so glad, your sister and nephews will also be pleased. Do you want to speak to your mother?” Mr. Simpson asked.

“No dad, actually it’s you I want to talk to,” Mario replied, sounding to his father as though he was a little confused.

“What’s up?” Mr. Simpson asked, now knowing it must be work-related because Mario would certainly not be divulging to him any matters of the heart. Those discussions were strictly reserved for his wife.

“I’m not sure I can do this job, dad. I’m a good detective but looking at all this paperwork, I’m not sure I can handle the bureaucracy or even if I want to,” Mario confessed.

“Of course you can son,” Mr. Simpson replied. “Anyway, what makes you think you can’t do it?” Mr. Simpson asked calmly.

“I’ve just returned from holiday and the paperwork in my in-tray, the voicemails, the emails, I’m never going to get through it,” Mario replied with some exasperation. After all those years working in the bank Mario knew that if anyone could handle all this crap, his father could.

“You know what son? Sometimes, when the phone is ringing, your pager is buzzing and someone is knocking at your door the best thing to do is just sit down and ignore it all. What you’re talking about here is even simpler. So, if you haven’t got one yet, grab a coffee, shut your office door and sit still for a moment enjoying your brew. Then, begin by going through your voicemails, short of people bursting unannounced through your door, they’re the most important means of communication. Snail mail can be deferred and emails are only electronic snail mail so they all take a lower priority. Of course, now you have the added distractions of texts and voice mails on your cellphone, but turn your phone off until you have caught up with everything else.

So, first, listen to each voice mail on your land-line and make a note of any that require action or follow-ups. I bet you'll find most of them are no longer valid. Delete each one after you have dealt with it. Next, go to the earliest of your emails and do much the same thing. Delete the crap informing you of retirements, office parties and the like, also those meeting notices of meetings that have already happened. The majority of the remainder probably don't affect you so file in appropriate folders or a reading file for future attention. Now, what few emails remain are manageable and you can schedule some time to deal with them at your leisure. Finally, go through each memo with the same approach. The crap and references to events that have happened, toss them. Future stuff, you put in your calendar and or a forward file, together with items that require action on your part. Your forward file should be organized by dates so that when you arrive at that date, necessary paperwork to be dealt with is at hand. Stuff that requires reading you put in a reading file and get to when you can. Now, if you're ruthless, I bet you can do all that in under an hour. People used to tell me that they spent the whole day catching up after returning from vacation, bullshit."

"You make it sound easy dad," Mario said laughing.

"It is easy, and remember this," Mr. Simpson paused, "my theory always was that it would take them at least six months to realize I couldn't do the job. By then, either you had got the hang of it or you were too far gone for them to get rid of you!"

Tuesday 18th December 2018

Chapter 11

Just after 8:00 AM Darlene appeared in the office and looked conspiratorially at Pete.

"Is that Mario in there?" Darlene whispered to Pete while she pointed to Mario's office.

"In living color," Pete replied.

"He wasn't expected back so soon! What's happened?" Darlene whispered.

"Don't know, he said he would tell me later," Pete said shaking his head until he realized Humph wasn't with her. "Where's Humph?"

"Getting your coffee," Darlene replied succinctly. "I decided that seeing as I am doing all his driving the least he could do was get the coffees once in a while."

"Quite right!" Pete replied. Just at that moment, the click of a stick on the floor could be heard as Humph approached precariously holding a paper tray of coffees. He too had noticed Mario in his office and just inclined his head to indicate that he was aware of the unexpected presence. As a result, there was pretty much silence in the room as each of them was having their own thoughts about Mario. Humph and Darlene were just hanging up their coats when they heard Mario's door opening and he strolled into their area.

The cut of the cloth on Mario's suit accentuated his slim, well-built physique. As his father used to tell him if you can't play the part at least look the part. But after what his father had just told him about carrying out his job duties he was beginning to wonder if his father had experienced confidence issues in his early days.

"Nice to see y'all bright and early," Mario began, as he stood there appearing a little nervous. "Now that we are all together, I will tell you why my trip has been unexpectedly truncated and I'm only going to tell you this once," Mario directed a look towards Darlene emphasizing his point. "Simply put, Magill and I decided our long-distance relationship was going to be a no-go. So, at the end of the first part of her tour, she decided to go back to Manchester for the holidays and I decided to return to New York. We parted amicably and we promised each other we would keep in touch but officially, we are no longer an item." Then, in a determined effort to deflect any questions he knew they all wanted to ask, especially Darlene, he immediately changed the subject - "so, what's happening with our latest case?"

There was a stunned silence for a few seconds. They had got to know Magill during their last case, the rest of the team loved her, and they all thought she and Mario had made a great couple. Darlene had a million questions to ask but Mario had made it abundantly clear that there was nothing further to discuss.

"Well, initially, all signs are that it appeared to have been an accident," Pete began, "but after interviewing the Great Grando's assistant, his name is Anton, he was adamant that Petr had sabotaged his own pyrotechnics and committed suicide."

"You said 'initially', but you don't sound as though you're fully convinced," Mario said.

"No, I'm not," Pete replied.

"Any other angles or suspects?" Mario asked.

"None, as yet," Pete replied, "but there's one other thing - we found a suicide note that appears to have been written by the victim."

"Darlene was telling me about that on the way in," Humph said. Offering his medical insight, he added, "if someone is a bit of a loner and it looks like his life's work is suddenly in jeopardy then he may feel he has nothing to live for. Another possibility is that maybe he had a medical condition, after all, he was in his mid-forties. No spring chicken to being flung from a cannon twice a day."

"As I said to Darlene," Pete countered, "it's all a little too convenient for my liking."

"But Pete, it all fits, look at the facts," Darlene argued, and she began counting off the facts with her fingers. "Everyone else in the circus is accounted for, so we have to assume the body is that of the Great Grando. Nobody else had access to the cannon area or was seen in the vicinity other than Anton or the Great Grando, and according to

Chuck, those explosives would have taken some preparation. No one else at the circus had that expertise."

"That we know of!" Pete countered.

"True," Darlene conceded, "but then there was the suicide note and the cleaning out of the bank accounts. From what we know he had no grievances with anyone, in fact, he was quite popular. Then there was his age, so suicide would check all the boxes."

"But there was no overcoat!" Pete simply said.

"What do you mean, no overcoat?" Mario asked looking confused.

"It's the middle of winter," Pete explained. "His luggage was all there, if he's committing suicide he's not going anywhere, hence his suitcase. But where are his winter coat, gloves and hat?"

"That's hardly grounds for disputing the outcome of his death," Humph chipped in, siding somewhat with Darlene. "He could have simply given them away or left them somewhere else."

"Then there's the computer that Anton said he always used to calculate his figures," Pete said. "That should be in his trailer but it's nowhere to be found. Why isn't it there?"

"He could have destroyed it, not wanting his trade secrets to fall into the wrong hands," Darlene suggested. But then Pete asked a question that drew silence from the others.

"But Anton was being earmarked to be his successor. What possible reason would there be for not letting him have the figures? Unless, of course, Anton has the computer in his possession!"

Tuesday 18th December 2018

Chapter 12

The others were all thinking of a counterargument to what Pete had just put forward but none of them could think of one.

“For now, let’s work on the possibility that the suicide note is bogus and continue with our investigation,” Mario suggested. He knew Pete’s observational skills and hunches only too well and if he didn’t think it was a suicide then there was an excellent chance that it wasn’t.

“But if there is a suicide note and it wasn’t suicide, then, logically, it must be murder! Why would there be a suicide note if it was an accident?” Humph asked.

“You’re absolutely right Humph,” Mario agreed. “The suicide note could have been written to throw us off the scent of the real killer, which is why we need Darlene to get a handwriting analysis carried out on the note.”

“Sure thing boss,” Darlene replied.

“I would also like to carry out some analysis on the remains of the victim, you know, just to confirm it is who we think it is,” Humph said.

“Good idea Humph, Pete, you and I will go and interview the Ringmaster and take another look around the scene,” Mario said.

“I’ll need to come with you to try and obtain some handwriting samples to compare with the note,” Darlene said.

The four of them piled into Mario’s squad car. Darlene was dying to know more about what had happened between Magill and Mario, but she knew this was not the time to ask anything. It wasn’t long before they arrived at the Gardens and Mario parked outside a cordoned-off area near the building and they walked into the arena. To their horror, the vehicle housing the burnt-out cannon had been removed but in doing so, the driver had appeared to have carried out a ten-point turn all over the crime scene and what precious little forensic evidence that had remained after the fire had now been just about obliterated by the reckless driver of the heavy-duty truck.

Tuesday 18th December 2018

Chapter 13

Pete was fuming and he asked a couple of nearby performers if they knew where Gwendoline was, they pointed back through the tunnel to her trailer. Pete turned and Mario saw the kind of mood that Pete was now in.

"Pete, let me handle this O.K.?" Mario said.

"But they've destroyed the crime scene, who told them they could get rid of that vehicle? We hadn't inspected it yet!" Pete said. Then he realized Mario was right, he was in no temperament to interview anyone, so he decided to return to what was left of the scene and join Humph to sift through the remaining debris.

Mario and Darlene went to find Gwendoline's trailer, which wasn't difficult to locate, it was the one where many of the circus performers were congregating. The two of them had to walk a gauntlet of performers to get to the trailer door, receiving disdained looks on their way. The trailer door was built in two halves, the bottom half was closed and the top half was open with the door clipped to the inside of the trailer. Mario knocked on the bottom half of the trailer door.

"Who is it and what do you want?" Came the sharp, angry, curt reply from Gwendoline.

“It’s Detectives Simpson and Knight, I believe you are expecting us,” Mario said gingerly after hearing her outburst from his knock on the door.

“Oh my goodness, I’m so sorry, come on in,” Gwendoline replied and came to the door to greet them and invite them into the trailer. “I’m sorry, I’m being bugged by the entertainers non-stop, I thought your knock on the door was just another one of them asking about something I couldn’t possibly answer until more information is available,” Gwendoline explained as she unclipped the top half of the door and closed the whole door to give them some privacy

“No problem, I understand,” Mario replied with a smile. Nobody had warned him that Gwendoline was such a tall, attractive woman. Standing beside him their eyes met at the same level, “my name is Detective Simpson; I am in charge of the team investigating the incident that occurred on Sunday.”

“Hi Detective Simpson, I’m Gwendoline, but I thought Detective Cannatelli was in charge,” she replied, holding out her hand in greeting. Gwendoline stood at approximately an inch or two shorter than Mario, although it was hard to tell with Mario’s hair. The unmistakable fact was that they were looking in each others’ eyes as Mario accepted her greeting. Darlene watched the scene unfold and thought the handshake lasted a little longer than would be professionally appropriate.

“Detective Cannatelli works for me. I was otherwise detained and had not expected to return until after the holidays but, circumstances have changed and here I am,” Mario explained.

“Well, I understand your detective doesn’t appear to think it was an accident,” Gwendoline stated.

“We’re investigating all possibilities,” Mario replied casually. “We were hoping to go over the crime scene today, but it appears the area has been compromised. Are you aware of who it was that gave the order to remove the cannon?”

“Oh no!” Gwendoline replied, wide-eyed with what appeared to be a genuine concern, “that would be me. The Fire Chief said they were all done with their investigations and the Garden’s cleaning staff were gung-ho to clear up the mess and asked us if we could remove the rig, which of course we did. Are you saying we shouldn’t have done that?”

“Typically, the fire department will do their research into the cause of the fire alongside our experts then our forensics teams can go to work before, we the detectives and the Medical Examiner get their shot at it,” Mario explained. “I don’t believe forensics had completed their investigations and we certainly hadn’t.”

“So, my poor decision may well hamper your investigation in determining what really happened, right?” Gwendoline asked.

"Well, it's not going to help, that's for sure," Mario replied, not trying to be too contrite about the situation, there was certainly nothing they could do about it now.

"Oh dear, if there's anything I can do," Gwendoline said as she slumped back down in her chair behind a desk that was swamped in papers and files. "Please, take a seat." At that moment, Gwendoline's cell phone rang, she took a quick look at the number, "I'm so sorry but I must take this call, it won't take long." While Gwendoline was on the phone, Mario took the opportunity to take a quick glance at the inside of the trailer before sitting down on an office chair in front of the desk in Gwendoline's trailer. The desk was strewn with paperwork and behind her on the wall of the trailer were numerous magnetic clips holding even more documentation, and he thought he had a problem with paperwork. There was also a rack of keys that also appeared to be held in place by a magnetic strip that was stuck to the metal wall of the trailer. Beside her desk was a safe that had been installed with a reinforced steel casing. He looked around at the rest of the trailer, the living area appeared to be tidy, if not full. He believed a realtor would classify it politely as 'busy'. As promised, Gwendoline's call didn't take long and once she had finished her call, she switched off her phone.

"Now, I can give you my full attention," Gwendoline said with a smile. Darlene had not responded to the invitation to sit and she was beginning to feel some chemistry happening between Mario and Gwendoline, so she decided to make an excuse for her exit.

"Look, pardon me but I need to check something out in Petr's trailer before going back to the scene of the accident. I'll explain the situation to the others," Darlene said, "meanwhile, I wonder if I may have Petr's trailer key once more please?"

"Oh sure," Gwendoline replied and reached around to a rack of keys that was fixed to the wall behind her. "There you go. Why don't you hang onto that? No one else is going to need it for the near future."

"Thanks, I'll leave you two to it then," Darlene said and with that and a knowing smile at Mario, she left the trailer.

"Where's the rig for the cannon now?" Mario asked.

"On its way to Greensburg, Pennsylvania," Gwendoline replied. "That's where the rig was originally made. We looked over the rig and after changing a couple of tires and removing the debris it was still roadworthy. We contacted the company to see if it was feasible to refit another cannon on the current base during our off-season. They agreed to take a look and if it can be fixed, they would provide a timeline for when it could be ready for next year's tour."

"So, who is driving it to Greensburg?" Mario asked.

"That would be Anton," Gwendoline replied. "The intention always was that Anton would one day take over the role of the human cannonball. If the cannon can be fixed, then the people at the company are going to set him up in a training program to bring him up to speed."

"Wow, the show must go on!" Mario said.

"Look detective, it may sound callous to you, but accidents happen all the time in this business. If we stopped an act every time an incident occurred there would be no circuses," Gwendoline replied candidly.

"I guess not," Mario replied. "By the way, please, call me Mario." Not sure of what to ask next so he reverted to one of the questions Pete had told him that he had asked yesterday, "I understand you are not aware of anyone who would want to see anything bad happen to Petr, is that correct?"

"Yes, at least nobody I know of. As I told your detective yesterday, Petr was very popular," Gwendoline replied.

"What about Anton? This has given him the opportunity he has always wanted," Mario asked, "could that have been a motive?"

"Anton? No, he doted on Petr and anyway, that kid hasn't got an ounce of malice in his body," Gwendoline replied emphatically.

Just at that moment, one of the performers was banging on Gwendoline's door with the panic du jour.

"Wait a minute please!" Gwendoline roared at the interloper, then turning back to Mario, "look, they're all worried about their futures. I know I told your detective that I would be free this morning, but I hadn't expected all this fallout. Can we meet over dinner tonight?

That would be the one place I could give you my full attention," Gwendoline asked.

"Sure, I can come by here, to pick you up, what time?" Mario asked.

"Shall we say 7:00?" Gwendoline asked with a smile.

"Absolutely, see you then," Mario said and left the trailer.

Once more, Mario walked back through the gauntlet of performers hanging around Gwendoline's trailer and returned to the arena. It didn't take long to find Pete and Humph at what was left of the crime scene. Mario noticed that Humph had retrieved some objects from the scene and had placed them into evidence bags. Mario had just missed Harry's team who had arrived to finish up with their investigations and were as surprised as Mario's team to see what was left of the scene. Her assistants had done their usual and looked around for a sight of Darlene. They had even asked Pete where she was, and they had shown disappointment when they found out that she was elsewhere.

"So, what did you find out?" Pete asked Mario.

"Not much, we got interrupted but I'm meeting her for dinner this evening to continue the questioning."

"Whoa, a date, goodbye Magill, hello Gwendoline," Darlene said as she walked up to join the group.

"It's not a date. She thought it would be the only place we could have a conversation without interruption," Mario replied tersely, then he went on to explain what little he had managed to discuss with the Ringmaster in the short time he was with her.

“So, we can’t ask Anton if he knows what happened to the Great Grando’s computer,” Pete said.

“We’ll have to put that one on the back burner for now,” Mario replied. “So, what have you managed to find out?”

“Well, I’m still leaning towards murder,” Pete replied.

“Despite the suicide note?” Mario asked.

“Despite the suicide note,” Pete confirmed as he nodded his head, “I think that was just an added prop to try and throw us off the scent.”

“But why?” Mario replied, “if the Great Grando was murdered why did he write a suicide note? I don’t understand!” Mario said.

“Darlene, did you manage to make a comparison on the handwriting?” Pete asked.

“You may not believe this, but apart from a couple of signatures on various ids., I couldn’t find a single handwritten piece of documentation anywhere in the trailer to compare it to,” Darlene replied.

“Convenient, don’t you think?” Pete said.

“Not if he was truly committing suicide. Why would it matter?” Darlene asked.

"It wouldn't," Pete replied, "but if it was murder, it's convenient that we can't compare the writing with anything in the trailer. So, we can't prove it was Petr's writing."

"We can't prove that it wasn't!" Darlene countered.

"So, if as you suspect it was murder, do you have any suspects in mind?" Mario asked Pete.

"Currently, I have two," Pete replied confidently, "Anton and your new girlfriend Gwendoline."

Tuesday 18th December 2018

Chapter 14

“She’s not my girlfriend,” Mario replied indignantly.

“But you’re going on a date with her tonight, right?” Darlene asked with a big smirk on her face.

“It’s not a date, it’s purely business. I need to ask her a few more questions, that’s all,” Mario explained.

“Like what?” Pete asked teasingly, knowing that currently, Mario had no more ideas than any of them.

“Well, I was hoping you could help me out with that,” Mario skated around the question. “What about you Humph? Did you find anything?”

“I found a knee bone that will probably suffice to provide sex and age determination, but judging by the state of the remains, that’s about the best I will be able to ascertain,” Humph replied dejectedly.

“We need to find out more about Anton and even Petr himself,” Pete told Mario. “Also, ask Gwendoline if anyone had joined the circus recently. Our man may not have been quite as popular with a new person.”

“Right, meanwhile, I had a thought, could you contact the photographer who took the picture that was on the front page of yesterday’s newspaper? He must have taken a slew of digital shots. You never know what we could glean from them,” Mario said to

Pete. “So, are we done here?” Mario asked. Everyone nodded their heads in agreement.

“O.K. let’s head back to the office,” Mario said.

By now it was well into the afternoon and Pete suggested a late lunch at a deli he knew in downtown Manhattan. They were all too familiar with Pete’s almost infinite knowledge of fine eateries and none of the others objected. As they walked back to the car, they could see a troupe of performers still gathered around Gwendoline’s trailer. It was a cold afternoon and they were all dressed in winter clothes. But Mario noticed that there was one person, a clown, who remained in his circus regalia, maintaining a little distance from the rest of the performers. The clown had a blue face with distinct white markings around the eyes. A blue, pointed hat sat jauntily on the side of the clown’s blue, smooth head which was most certainly covered with a bald cap. The tuxedo-styled costume had blue and white stripes and a dickey bow-tie completed the ensemble. The bulbous outfit was billowing with the slight, albeit cold breeze that was in the air. He was also wearing typical clown-type oversized shoes that must have been about two-feet long and were painted the same color blue as his face. Amongst all the other performers who were dressed in their normal street clothes, the clown appeared a little out of place. Mario mentioned it to the other members of his team but none of them placed too much emphasis on the idiosyncrasy of the clown. Mario pushed that thought to the back of his mind, for now. That was another thing he would be asking Gwendoline later, over dinner.

Tuesday 18th December 2018

Chapter 15

After lunch, Mario drove everyone back to the office where he continued to sort through his backlog of paperwork in disbelief of how much more it had grown during the short time he had been out of the office since he had left that morning. Pete began hunting down the news reporter to obtain his photographs while Darlene drove Humph to his lab. to carry out analysis on the bone fragments he had bagged at the crime scene and the evidence Harry had forwarded the previous day.

That evening, Mario drove to the Gardens, parked in the private enclosure and walked over to Gwendoline's trailer. Surprisingly, there were still a few of the circus's troupe hanging around Gwendoline's trailer. He muttered a couple of polite 'excuse me' phrases as he approached the door and tapped lightly while shouting 'Detective Simpson'. He thought that may obtain a better response than the initial one he had experienced earlier in the day.

"Coming,' came the reply from Gwendoline and sure enough, the door opened revealing Gwendoline dressed in a beautiful red dress that accentuated her perfect figure. She also wore heeled black shoes, not too high though. Her long blonde hair hung down across her shoulders. Mario thought she looked striking. Darlene's words suddenly came back to him, *'goodbye Magill, hello Gwendoline'*. She reached around the door to grab her coat to put it on before climbing gingerly down the grated trailer steps and locking her door.

"I hope you don't mind, I've already chosen where we are going. There's a small restaurant called Ballotelli's on 5th Avenue that my family traditionally frequented when we're performing in town. Do you know it?" Gwendoline asked.

"Can't say that I have heard of it," Mario replied.

"It's a great little place, you'll love it" Gwendoline replied.

"You mentioned that you always frequent it when you are in New York, why is that?" Mario was curious to know.

"I'll tell you why on the way there," Gwendoline quickly replied because a chorus of questions from members of the circus troupe hit her as she began to lead Mario away from her trailer.

To Mario, it seemed akin to a meeting of the United Nations, as Gwendoline was being bombarded with questions in multiple languages which she appeared to be answering in kind. She stopped for a few seconds to address them all and then turned on her heels to leave.

"Whoa, that wasn't so bad, I've had worse," Gwendoline said, relieved that she had managed to satisfy her staff, at least for now.

"My, you speak a lot of languages," Mario said, "impressive."

"Well, when you've grown up around circus performers from all over the world you pick up enough to get by," Gwendoline replied casually. "Look, leave your car, parking can be a pain outside the restaurant, let's grab a cab, we'll be there in ten minutes."

Mario hailed a cab and during their journey, Gwendoline explained the reason for choosing this particular restaurant.

"The owners are Italian and they arrived here just before the second world war. Originally the whole family were circus performers and actually worked for my grandfather, but Francesco, that was the original owner, well, he got injured during the war, and afterward he could no longer function as an acrobat, so he opened a restaurant."

"But it can't be Francesco who still runs the place, surely!" Mario said.

"Well, yes and no," Gwendoline replied with a beautiful, mischievous, grin that Mario hadn't seen before. "It is Francesco but obviously not ***the*** Francesco, it is the grandson who now runs the restaurant. The original Francesco died a number of years ago."

The cab pulled up outside a small, nicely maintained restaurant with the name 'Ballotelli's' on top of a large picture window with partially opened lace curtains hanging from a brass rail. It looked like a typical Italian restaurant, in fact, it appeared to Mario like something out of a Godfather movie. He'd lived in New York all his life and being half-Italian, he couldn't understand how he hadn't heard of this place before.

As they entered the restaurant, they were greeted by a well-dressed maître d' who instantly recognized Gwendoline and immediately clasped his hands and shouted out 'Francesco', much to the surprise of the other patrons in the dining-room. There was even a small tear running down his cheek. As quick as Francesco could run from the kitchen, where he had been supervising meal preparations, he was there hugging Gwendoline like long-lost friends. After much continental kissing and introductions from other members of the family, Mario was finally introduced, although he felt very much like an afterthought. Mario was in doubt whether he was going to be able to receive the privacy he needed to ask his questions.

Eventually, they were shown to a table which, as it turned out, was secluded and outside the hearing range of anyone else. After they were seated and their drinks order taken, they were finally left alone for the first time.

"I guess you'd better begin asking any questions you have now, I don't think you will have much time later," Gwendoline whispered to him.

"No kidding," Mario replied, "I guess they think the world of you!"

"My grandfather helped them out financially to get their business going, so their family never forgot that," Gwendoline replied, just before the drinks arrived.

"Wow, that was very generous of your grandfather," said Mario. Then he decided to follow Gwendoline's advice and begin with his questions. "O.K., so what can you tell me about Petr and Anton?"

"Well, Petr had been with us for about five years. I have never had a problem with him. He joined our circus because he felt he could provide an exciting attraction with the human cannonball act, which we hadn't included in our performances for years. The rig was sitting idle, he had somehow heard about it and after a few trial runs we agreed to take him on."

"Did you carry out a background check on him? What had he been doing before he joined your circus?" Mario asked.

"We don't do a background check on anyone if you mean like a criminal record or something like that. We usually know the acts we hire, their reputation precedes them," Gwendoline explained. "In Petr's case, we had never heard of him, but he gave us the name of the circus he had been with before coming to us. I contacted them and they gave me a flowering report, so I hired him."

"Which circus was it?" Mario asked.

"I forget the name but it was a small European outfit that I had never heard of. They toured around the Balkans so it was not surprising that I was not aware of them," Gwendoline replied. "Petr had given me the owner's phone number and I contacted him."

"Did he give a reason as to why he left the previous circus?" Mario was curious to know.

"Simple, they folded," Gwendoline said casually. "This is a fickle business and they were very much into the animal acts. As you know, animals in circuses have become passé. 'Cirque du Soleil' paved the way for a new brand of circus entertainment that was in line with the public's thinking about the treatment of caged animals. Case in point, 'Circus of America' was late to adjust and they went bankrupt, as did a few other outfits. We inherited a few acts, as did other surviving circuses and Petr was part of the collateral damage."

"Do you know where he came from, originally?" Mario asked.

"He once told me he came from Macedonia and he left there in the nineties just before all the troubles started," Gwendoline said. "He felt there was going to be a war when all the countries in the region began to go independent."

"Well he got that right," Mario said.

"As for Anton," Gwendoline continued, "he also came to us about five years ago, although a few months after Petr had joined us. Anton was just looking for work. He'd arrived in the states from Europe. He had no job, no roof over his head and no money. Petr had been complaining that he needed an assistant, so I let Petr interview him. They seemed to click from the get-go."

"One other question I was asked to present to you, you've said Petr got on well with everyone, has there been any new additions to your troupe that may not have taken a liking to him?" Mario asked.

"Only old Limpy who joined us when we first arrived in New York," Gwendoline answered with a smile, after thinking about the question for a few seconds.

"Limpy?" Mario asked.

"Limpy is the clown with the blue face, you may have seen him hanging around," Gwendoline replied, "although I believe he has spent most of his time since the accident in his trailer. He only joined us just in time for the performances at the Gardens."

"Ah, that's another question I have for you," Mario just recalled his earlier observation, "why does he continue to remain in costume?"

"He's a natural and that's his way of trying to keep everyone's spirits up. This was a devastating accident that hit everyone hard, usually, we're really one big, happy family," Gwendoline said, trying to justify the clown's actions.

"Funny though, he was standing a little away from the rest of the performers waiting around your trailer," Mario said a little curiously.

"That's because he doesn't know the other performers too well, so he probably wanted to keep a little distance between them," Gwendoline responded.

"It must take him ages just to put those shoes on every day and tie up the laces," Mario remarked, but Gwendoline just laughed.

"Ha, they're just false shoe-laces," Gwendoline explained. "He has real shoes on his feet and the clown shoes go on top just like galoshes. On and off in an instant."

"Oh, I see," Mario mused. "So what's his history?" Mario asked.

"Limpy has been bumping from circus to circus in North America for quite a few years. His last gig had finished for the season, so he just came along for the ride," Gwendoline said. "I knew of him, of course, us circus people are a very esoteric group, keep ourselves very much to ourselves. Hell, we're almost incestuous, families marry into other circus families. Even young Francesco here got hitched with the daughter of a family in our circus who had a trapeze act. I believe she works here in the background doing the accounting."

"Probably juggling the books then," Mario quipped.

"Oh, very funny," Gwendoline said but she was genuinely laughing.

"But you've never married, have you?" Mario asked almost shyly.

"Too busy, my father had a stroke a few years ago. He's fine now but I am an only child, so I became the boss. Wasn't a stretch really, my mother died in a circus-related accident when I was quite young," Gwendoline paused for a second, obviously reminiscing about her mother, but she didn't dwell too long on the topic and she didn't elaborate further. "So, I was brought up by my father and the rest of the circus performers, as I said, we are a close family. The reality is, I had been unwittingly groomed to run the circus my whole life, so no, no room for marriage, I'm afraid," Gwendoline explained to Mario although he detected a little semblance of regret in her voice.

"So, going back to the topic of your clown, why the name, Limpy?" Mario asked getting back to his investigative duties.

"Have you seen him walk?" Gwendoline asked in surprise, returning to her normal, happy, self, "if you had you'd know why. He's originally from Bosnia. He was an army officer, ciphers I think, and was seriously injured during a bomb attack during the war. He nearly lost his leg, they had to reconstruct it, so now he has a permanent limp. While he was in the hospital, he would visit the children's ward to cheer them up. He soon realized that he had a penchant for making children laugh so he decided to become a clown instead of returning to his job as an accountant. He traveled with various circuses in Europe before coming to the States a few years ago. Limpy even has an egg in the clown registry, has had one for many years."

"An egg in the clown registry?" Mario asked, totally dumbfounded, "I think you are going to have to help me out with that one."

"Well, when a clown, such as Limpy, has been around for a while, a photograph of his unique make-up is sent to the International Clown Registry. A likeness is painted on a ceramic egg and that serves as a copyright to the clown's unique face." Gwendoline explained with all seriousness.

"You're kidding me right?" Mario asked, not knowing whether she was serious or just egging him on.

"Absolutely not," Gwendoline replied sincerely, "there's a museum in London that you can visit if you don't believe me." Mario was unsure about that one, but he didn't need to pursue it, so he changed tracts.

"Does either Petr or Limpy have any family?" Mario asked.

"Petr, I don't know much else about him, he kept his personal life very private. I had never heard him mention the existence of any family," Gwendoline explained but then her face saddened, "as for Limpy, he had a wife and three children. They were all murdered in the Srebrenica massacre in 1995, while he was hospitalized. They didn't tell him about their deaths until he was almost recovered, they were concerned about suicide."

"That's sad," Mario said, but inwardly, he was beginning to believe the presence of two men from the same war-torn area of the world was a bit too much of a coincidence for his liking.

Tuesday 18th December 2018

Chapter 16

Once the drinks had been served and the dinner ordered, questions regarding the investigation had to be dispensed with. Francesco regularly visited their table to make sure everything was perfect. Mario was beginning to have a difficult time considering that Gwendoline was a potential murder suspect, but he knew Pete wouldn't relent considering the current availability of the facts. After all, Gwendoline had been the one to issue the order to repair the vehicle and have Anton drive it away.

As Francesco and Gwendoline flip-flopped between speaking English and Italian, Mario had not let on that he also spoke both languages fluently. Although, with a name like Mario he would have thought one of them would catch on. Nevertheless, there was nothing bad spoken about him or anything else in the exchange between the two long-lost friends, it was all friendly banter. Francesco was not a tall guy, but he had a lithe, athletic-looking body which Mario suspected, based on the family's history of acrobats, was that he was an extremely strong man. Others that worked at the restaurant also had similar builds, all relatively handsome with dark hair and dark eyes, possibly brothers or cousins. Mario had the feeling that the restaurant didn't need to employ any bouncers.

At the end of the meal, Mario offered to pay the bill but Gwendoline insisted it was her idea and that she would be paying. Before a resolution could be decided upon, both of them were trumped by Francesco who told them that their money was no good in his restaurant. He was so insistent he brought them both digestifs in the form of snifters of brandy in antique, crystal, brandy glasses.

"After all the wine and now this brandy I'm drinking, I'm not sure I will be legal to drive home," Mario stated.

"You don't have to," Gwendoline replied, giving him that mischievous look once more and eyeing him sexily as she did so. "I won't be returning to the trailer to-night, I have a hotel room booked for the next few nights. It just happens to be right around the corner."

Wednesday 19th December 2018

Chapter 17

The next morning, Mario arrived in the office a little late and wearing the same clothes that he had worn the previous day, a point which did not go unnoticed by Darlene. Mario gave the team a summary of the discussion he'd had with Gwendoline especially about the circumstances in which Petr and Limpy joined the circus.

"She told me about Limpy being on an egg in some museum somewhere, which I thought was a bit far-fetched," Mario said with a wave of his hand as if he was disposing of the information.

"Oh, the Clown Egg Registry in Dalston. Wow, Limpy is in that? Impressive!" Pete replied.

"You've heard of it?" Mario asked amazed. "How do you know this shit, Pete?"

"I've been there, it's in London. I was a big circus fan growing up. My mother took me there during one of our trips to England," Pete explained. Mario just shook his head wondering if there was anything Pete didn't know.

After answering a few more questions to clarify some details, he then asked them how they were doing with their investigations.

"What's happening with what you're all investigating?" Mario asked.

"I carried out some tests on that knee-bone I found yesterday," Humph replied.

"And?" Mario asked.

"It's consistent with the age and sex of Petr," Humph replied, "but there is nothing else I can glean from it."

"Would any of Harry's team's photos be of any use?" Mario asked.

"I doubt it, but it wouldn't do any harm to take a look through them, I guess," Humph replied reluctantly.

"Darlene, contact those photographers on Harry's team and see if you can get copies of their photographs sent to us," Mario said.

"Sure thing boss," Darlene replied derisively, not relishing the thought of talking to those smarmy photographers.

"Pete, what about you?" Mario asked.

"Well, I've been scanning the photographs I received from the newspaper guy. There's a couple of inconsistencies I'd like explained," Pete replied.

"Such as?" Mario asked.

"Well, take a look at this one. It was taken the day before the accident," Pete said, turning his monitor so that Mario could see it. "Here's the Great Grando, helmet off, waving to the crowd during the introduction of all the performers at the beginning of the show. But on the day of the accident, he's not out there with the other performers. The other funny thing is that in a photograph just before the human cannonball act, see, right here," Pete said pointing to the Great Grando being introduced, "his helmet is off and he is holding it as he is waving his arms. But when he was introduced on the day of the accident, he waved, but his helmet never came off his head."

"So, what's the significance of that?" Mario asked.

"I don't know, that's what I want to find out," Pete said. "It may be a red herring, it may mean something, I just don't know."

"Well, I'm seeing Gwendoline later, I'll ask her about it," Mario said.

"Another date?" Darlene asked mischievously.

"No Darlene, I have some follow-up questions for her," Mario replied with a little exasperation at the seemingly infinite jibes he was receiving from his female detective. "Would you like to come with me?"

"Sure, when are we leaving?" Darlene quickly replied, more interested to witness the chemistry between the recently introduced couple, now that they had been on a date and what seemed like so much more.

"By the way, where did you end up eating last night?" Pete asked.

"A place called Ballotelli's on -," Mario began but was quickly interrupted by Pete.

"On 5th, great restaurant. It has all those pictures of famous performers on the walls," Pete said, "I love that place."

"How do you know this shit, Pete?" Mario asked, now beginning to get really frustrated with Pete. "Is there a restaurant, diner, deli or food truck in this city that you don't know?"

“Whoa, steady there boss, just saying,” Pete replied almost apologetically with his hands up as though he was warding off the verbal assault. “Again, because I was such a big circus fan growing up, my mother used to take me there as a treat sometimes.”

“I bet it was a treat for you last night too, huh?” Darlene said to Mario with a big smile on her face.

“O.K., enough of this, I have work to do. Let’s cut out in an hour for those who want to come,” Mario said and returned to his office leaving the others giving conspirative smiles to each other.

Mario had always kept a change of clothes in his locker for emergency purposes, the only difference now that he was chief was it was situated in a wardrobe in the office he had inherited from old Horowitz. He also kept a toiletry bag containing some personal hygiene items. He gathered up everything and went down to the change rooms in the basement of the building where there were also showers where he could clean up and change into his spare clothes. In retrospect, he wished he had gone straight to his office and done this before speaking to the others.

While he was in the shower Mario contemplated the events of the previous evening. There was no doubt in his mind sparks had flown between him and Gwendoline, but was this romance going to be long-lasting, or was it just another fling?

While Mario was taking his shower, Chuck appeared in the office. He greeted everyone and congratulated them on being assigned the case.

“We’re just off to the circus,” Darlene said to Chuck, “do you want to come?”

“No, I think I’ve got everything I need. Any idea about who did it?” Chuck asked as he plonked himself down on the desk Mario used to use before his promotion.

“There was a suicide note,” Darlene replied, “but Pete isn’t buying it.”

“Nor am I,” Chuck replied hastily. “I know the other day I said that the explosion would have caused a quick death, but I’ve been giving it some thought. Whoever set that fire would also have known that there was always the possibility of something going wrong. Not only could it have been a slow agonizing death it may have resulted in just extremely bad injuries. Regardless, those explosives were set up by an expert. No, that was no suicide.”

“The other possibility is Anton,” Pete added, happy that Chuck was endorsing his murder theory. “He had the means and a motive.”

“Not for me, too young and inexperienced,” Chuck replied shaking his head. “I met Anton just after the fire was extinguished and I began looking at what was left. Sure, he could probably have put together a dirty bomb from instructions on the internet, but whoever set that up to look like an accident was experienced in timed detonations and explosives. I would have to say it was an ex-military man. I doubt that Anton is your murderer, although, I agree, you can't rule him out."

"What about where the explosives came from? You said the other day that they're not exactly the type of thing you can buy in stores," Pete said.

"Still looking into that," Chuck replied, "but I have to warn you we may never get an answer to that. The last time I saw incendiaries like those was when I was in Bosnia. I was seconded there as part of the United Nations Task Force together with a detachment of Canadian Mounted police and forces from other countries." Just at that moment, Mario returned to the office and managed to catch what Chuck had just said.

"Wait a minute!" Mario said, "last night Gwendoline told me that Limpy had been an officer during the Bosnian conflict."

"Well, I would have thought that's a lead worth pursuing," Chuck replied as he stood up, "anyway, this won't do, places to go, people to see, I'll catch you later. Good luck at the circus." With that, Chuck left the office while the others digested this new snippet of information.

When Mario returned to his office, he sifted through some of the paperwork that old Chief Horowitz used to protect his team from. Now that he was forced to deal with it himself, he vowed that if he ever got to the top this all had to be streamlined. But in reality, he knew that every cop in his position had said the very same thing, yet still nothing changed. In between clearing the paperwork in his inbox, he had tried calling Gwendoline a couple of times but had received no reply. Did that answer the question of whether his new relationship was just a fling or was she otherwise occupied? Mario decided to drop the paperwork and go visit Gwendoline immediately. He was about to leave his office when the phone rang. The call display revealed it was the Commissioner, he decided he had better take the call.

"Detective Simpson," Mario said succinctly.

"Ah, Simpson, I'd heard you had returned," the Commissioner replied, but without any further questioning regarding his early return from vacation, he drove straight to the point. "How is the investigation going regarding that accident at the Gardens? I was hoping it would be over by now."

"Afraid not sir," Mario replied with some apprehension, "we believe it may be a murder investigation we are now conducting."

"What?" The Commissioner shouted down the phone, "I was under the impression that this was merely an accident."

"We believe it's a little more than that sir," Mario said bowing his head in his hand in frustration as he began to explain the situation to the Commissioner. This was the first time Mario had to experience a one-on-one discussion with the man and not for the first time, he was beginning to understand the job Chief Horowitz had done protecting his detectives from this onslaught of unnecessary hassles.

"Well, get to the bottom of this as soon as possible and whatever you do, don't let the press know about your suppositions. Until you've solved the case, as far as they are concerned, it was an accident. Have you got that Simpson?" The Commissioner demanded.

"Absolutely sir," Mario said as the line went dead.

Mario left his office, his voluminous hair still wet from his shower and walked into the adjoining office.

"Right, who's coming?" Mario shouted as though he meant business. There was no reply but there was a shuffling of chairs as the three other members of his team rose from their seated positions. They traveled down the elevator to Mario's car and he drove to the Gardens to talk with Gwendoline.

On the way, Pete filled Mario in on the rest of what was discussed during Chuck's visit, but it didn't change the facts, Limpy was now placed firmly at the top of the list of suspects. Surprisingly, on arrival at Gwendoline's trailer, she was nowhere to be found, nor did there appear to be anyone else in the vicinity. Eventually, they located one of the performers who directed them to the inside of the arena. Inside the arena, all the performers and Gwendoline could be seen walking between separate rows of seats looking for something.

As soon as Gwendoline saw Mario and his team, she ran to an aisle and rushed down the steps towards him.

“Boy, am I glad to see you,” an obviously distressed Gwendoline said as she came running up to Mario and hugged him.

“Why? What’s wrong?” Mario asked with some concern.

“It’s Shorty, he’s disappeared,” Gwendoline replied before bursting out in tears.

Wednesday 19th December 2018

Chapter 18

"Gwendoline, slow down, who's Shorty, and what makes you think he has disappeared?" Mario asked as he released Gwendoline from their embrace.

"Shorty is the little guy, you must have seen him around. You know every circus has a little person, we call him Shorty, we're not always creative with names in this business," Gwendoline replied trying to bravely bring a little humor to the situation as she looked at the others with a forced smile.

"Could he have decided he'd had enough and just took off?" Pete asked.

"No, no way. I've known Shorty all my life. We grew up together in this circus, his family was an act for years. He's like a brother to me," Gwendoline explained. "He wouldn't have left without telling me. For two reasons, first, he hadn't been paid yet and secondly, he was going to accompany me in my car as we all took the drive back to Florida for the winter break."

"So, you've no idea where he could be?" Mario asked.

"No, none," Gwendoline replied.

"So, why are you checking between the rows of seats?" Pete asked.

"Well, Shorty has been known to go on a bender now and again and crashes-out in peculiar places, but he hasn't done that in years," Gwendoline explained.

"Could he have left the Gardens and gone to a bar somewhere downtown?" Darlene asked.

"No, he would never have gone out alone and everyone else is accounted for," Gwendoline replied.

"When was Shorty last seen?" Pete asked.

"When you and I left last night," Gwendoline replied, nodding her head towards Mario. "It appears everyone dispersed and a couple of the performers saw Shorty heading towards Limpy's trailer."

"You told me that Limpy hadn't been here long. Had they struck up a friendship?" Mario asked.

"It's possible, they had to coordinate a few routines together so they had been rehearsing and got to know each other," Gwendoline replied, but then her face scrunched up a little before she added, "although now that I think about it, one of the performers did say that since entering Limpy's trailer nobody has seen Shorty since."

"Have you spoken to Limpy about it?" Pete asked.

"No, he's already left," Gwendoline replied. "I paid him just before you arrived for our dinner date last night. Limpy told me he would be leaving for Florida early this morning and we agreed that he would contact me in the new year to discuss joining next year's tour."

"You paid him?" Mario questioned her, "you mean like cash?"

"Yes, cash. With a few exceptions, all my circus staff gets paid by cash," Gwendoline replied before continuing with an explanation. "You have to remember most of the people who work in the circus are foreigners and only a few of them have their green cards. The less the government knows the better, so paying them cash is best for everyone concerned. For example, Petr was legal and he had been with us for several years so he was paid directly into his bank account. In Limpy's case, although he was legal, he had only joined us recently and was not expected to be with us long, so he was paid cash." Then a thought suddenly came to Gwendoline. "Oh my God, you don't think Limpy is responsible for anything that may have happened to Shorty do you?"

"Do you have a photo id. of Limpy, one that we can use to put out to alert all the police departments?" Pete asked casually.

Wednesday 19th December 2018

Chapter 19

"What makes you think Limpy could have harmed Shorty?" Gwendoline asked with a hint of desperation in her voice.

"We think it may be possible that Limpy is responsible for Petr's death," Mario replied, "maybe Shorty knows something he shouldn't."

"What on earth would make you think that?" Gwendoline asked.

"Limpy is an ex-army officer who participated in the Bosnian war and it is possible the incendiary explosives that caused the accident are of the same type used during that conflict," Pete replied. "Maybe Shorty was somehow on to him."

"But why would Limpy have killed Petr?" Gwendoline asked.

"We don't know that yet," Mario replied, "but if we could get photos of Limpy and Petr we can contact other policing agencies and we may be able to obtain an answer." They walked over to Gwendoline's trailer and she rummaged through her files for the photographs. While she was searching, Mario continued with his questioning.

"Look Gwendoline, I know how distressing this must be for you, but I must ask you a couple of questions," Mario stated.

"Sure, go ahead," Gwendoline said resignedly.

"We were reviewing some of the photographs a newspaper reporter took that begged answers," Mario explained. "We noticed that during Saturday's performance, 'The Great Grando' was there during the introduction of all the performers but at Sunday's performance he wasn't in attendance. Can you explain that?" Gwendoline looked pensive for a moment as she thought back to those two days that already seemed so long ago. Gwendoline had found the photographs she had been looking for and handed them to Mario.

"Oh, of course, I remember now," Gwendoline replied. "On Saturday the cannonball act was the last of our performances and on Sunday it was the first. Let me explain, remember when there used to be lions and tigers in the circuses?" Mario nodded. "Well, there used to be a lot of work setting up the cages. They would make the cats the last act on the card so that the cages would be ready for the first act during the next day's performance. Well it's the same procedure with the human cannonball act, we have to set up the catching net, so, last act, first act."

"Makes sense, but that doesn't explain why Petr wasn't there," Mario said, looking a little perplexed.

"Because he needed those extra minutes to do his calculations and final checks," Gwendoline replied. "That was not unusual."

"I see, so that explains that but I have another question," Mario said. "We noticed in the photos that during the Saturday performance Petr's helmet was off before he began his act, but on Sunday it remained on. Any reason for that?"

"No idea," Gwendoline replied with a quizzical look. "You have to remember, I'm usually in the center of the ring and Petr's entrance would be behind me. I really didn't ever take much notice of such idiosyncrasies. What significance do you think that would have on the case?"

"Not sure, if anything, I was just hoping you might know the answer," Mario said.

Pete arrived with the news that Shorty was nowhere to be found which brought on another round of tears from Gwendoline.

"Did Limpy have a car?" Pete asked.

"Yes, he did. I don't have the make or plate number but I'm sure the Garden's security would have made a note of it," Gwendoline replied. Pete left them to visit the Garden's security office.

"He's probably half-way to Florida by now and what if he is responsible for Shorty's disappearance?" Gwendoline asked as she began to reminisce about her memories with the little man. "When we were kids, Shorty and I would spend our days visiting all the acts as they practiced their routines. We would join in and learn all the basic moves. As we got older, we both became good enough to fill in if any of the performers were injured, sick or pregnant, which happened a lot. In the circus we have no prejudices, so Shorty was just one of us, but outside…." Her voice trailed off and she snapped out of her reverie with another bout of crying.

Mario spent the rest of the day consoling Gwendoline while Pete put out a search to all the police departments for Limpy's vehicle. According to the Garden's security, Limpy had left the compound at 3:35 in the morning. There was a note beside the entry stating that the driver was leaving to get an early start on his trip to Florida, which was consistent with what Gwendoline had told them. Pete also sent the security id. photographs, physical descriptions of Limpy and Petr, given to him by Gwendoline, to the F.B.I. to see if they had anything on the two men. Meanwhile, Darlene and Humph had helped in a fruitless search for Shorty but it was beginning to appear that Limpy was the only one with any answers.

Early the next morning, Mario left Gwendoline's hotel room only to be greeted by a newspaper vendor displaying the daily's headlines:

'DEATH AT THE GARDENS NOT AN ACCIDENT'

Thursday 20th December 2018

Chapter 20

This morning Mario had not made the same mistake he had made the previous day. This morning he had showered before leaving Gwendoline's hotel room and had changed into clean clothes that he had retrieved earlier during a quick visit to his home and had left in his car. On arrival at his desk, Mario didn't have to wait long before the Commissioner was calling him on the phone.

"What the hell is going on here Simpson? I specifically told you to keep this investigation out of the press," the Commissioner did not appear to be happy. "My God Simpson, a simple request on a simple investigation and now it is all over the media."

"Yes sir, I take responsibility for that," Mario replied meekly. "We asked a reporter to forward a copy of the photographs to us that he had taken at the circus, and I guess he put two and two together. My fault, I should have told him to keep stum – I didn't think, it won't happen again sir."

"See that it doesn't," the Commissioner said as though he accepted the explanation and apology before abruptly hanging up. This response surprised Mario, maybe he was beginning to learn how to deal with the Commissioner after all.

By 9:30 that morning the team was meeting in the office, mulling over what little information they had when they received a surprise visit from Harry. Rather than send an email, she had brought over a CD containing all the forensic team's photographs from the crime scene and she handed it to Darlene, who was much relieved to see that she hadn't brought along her two ogling photographers. Harry had also carried out some analysis on the suicide letter Darlene and Pete had found in Petr's trailer and confirmed that only Petr's fingerprints had been on both the envelope and the letter.

"So, it's beginning to look a lot like suicide then?" Harry asked.

"Well, we've had a development," Mario replied.

"Oh yeah, what's that then?" Harry asked.

"One of the clowns has gone missing, you know, the little fellow," Mario said.

"I remember seeing him," Harry said.

"Well, according to Gwendoline, he would never leave the confines of the circus and he was going to be traveling south with her," Mario explained before continuing, "what's more, the clown that walked with a limp has also taken off."

"So, that's just coincidence, surely," Harry said with her arms outstretched in a 'so what' gesture.

"Except that according to Chuck he believes the incendiaries used during the fire were of the type used during the Bosnia conflict and Limpy is Bosnian," Mario explained.

"An ex-army officer to boot," Pete added.

"Yes, but Gwendoline said he worked in ciphers, not with bombs," Mario countered.

"Or at least that's what he had told Gwendoline," Pete suggested.

"Playing devil's advocate here but again, that's just another coincidence, circumstantial evidence weighed up against the concrete evidence that points to suicide," Harry offered. "What else have you got?"

"No overcoat," Darlene said.

"No overcoat? Whose overcoat?" Harry asked looking totally bewildered.

"No overcoat," Pete replied with some forcefulness. "Why was there no cold-weather clothing in the Great Grando's trailer?" Harry thought for a moment and sat her slight frame on Pete's desk as she thought that one through.

"I see," Harry said to herself. After another moment's thought, she added, "so you're thinking that it's all intentionally pointing to suicide."

"You got it!" Pete replied.

"And you think it's this Limpy that killed first the Great Grando and now, possibly, the little fellow," Harry surmised.

"Right again," Pete replied as he nodded his head. But then Harry thought of something else.

“So how the hell did Limpy get the Great Grando to write out a suicide note?”

Thursday 20th December 2018

Chapter 21

"We don't know for sure that the Great Grando did or didn't write the note, we have nothing to compare it to," Pete replied, "and as for the note if Limpy used gloves then there would still only be the Great Grando's prints on the envelope and paper."

"I see," mused Harry. She was figuring that everything pointed to suicide, but, like Mario, she was also only too aware of Pete's intuitions, she knew him better than anyone in the room. "I guess you won't know for sure until you find this Limpy guy."

"I agree," said Mario. "Did you extend the search to out-of-state Pete?"

"Sure did," Pete replied, "and Homeland Security along the Canadian border."

"So, you really think the killer is Limpy?" Darlene asked Pete. "Everyone else I have spoken to around the circus felt he was a gentle soul, although they hadn't known him long. Not one of them thought he was capable of murder."

"I'm just saying I don't think it was a suicide," Pete replied. "Beyond that, I don't have enough facts to make a decision on whether Limpy is a killer or not."

"And Shorty?" Darlene asked.

"We don't know for certain that he is missing. We just haven't found him yet," Pete replied. "As Harry said, it could be just coincidence."

Just then Pete's phone rang and the call-id displayed 'F.B.I.', Pete answered it.

"Cannatelli here," Pete said as he put his phone on speaker.

"Hey Pete, Simmons here," the voice crackled through the speaker-phone. "I've checked out the two ids. that you sent me. Ahmed Isaković is indeed who he says he is, an ex-Bosnian army officer who arrived in the states in 1995. Originally, he settled in New York then St. Louis where there is a big Bosnian community. After a couple of years he began traveling the country doing what he's doing now, performing as a clown."

"Anything in your files that indicate what he did during the conflict?" Pete asked.

"Yes, he was a Cryptographer," Simmons replied. "Apparently he was a bit of a math wizard, that's why he was given the position." Pete looked up at the others as everything they knew about Limpy was being confirmed and shaking their very foundations of him being a murderer.

"What about Petr Stojanovski?" Pete asked.

"That one is a bit more difficult," Simmons replied. "No hits on the name so we're running his photo through Interpol's face recognition system to see if anything comes up. Should be a day or two before we get any results."

"Great, thanks for your help," Pete replied and turned the speaker off.

"So, the person we think is a murderer has been identified but the name of the person who has been murdered is not in the F.B.I.'s files," Pete said looking down at a pencil he was absentmindedly twirling in his hand. "Don't you find that a little strange?"

"In what way?" Darlene asked, but before Pete could reply his phone rang again. This time a number was being displayed that he didn't recognize, he picked up the receiver.

"Cannatelli here," Pete said. The others waited while Pete listened to whoever it was on the other end of the line and watched as Pete began writing down details.

"Great work pal but whatever you do, don't touch the vehicle," Pete said. "We're coming right now." Pete hung up the phone and addressed the group.

"They've located Limpy's car in a long-term car park at LaGuardia airport."

Thursday 20th December 2018

Chapter 22

"Darlene, contact Chuck at the bomb squad and tell him to get his team out to meet us at the multi-story car park at LaGuardia. Here, take this," Pete ordered and ripped off the piece of paper from the pad on which he had written down the car's details and location. "Give him the car's description, I want the vehicle checked for explosives before we start investigating it."

"Sure, skipper," Darlene said, and she strode quickly across to her desk to make the call.

"Well, time for me to leave you to it," Harry said. "If you need me, you know my number." With that, she gave a brisk wave as she left the office. Humph began to struggle to his feet to don his coat. Mario was about to return to his office to grab his coat when he thought of something else.

"Pete, before we leave, get onto airport security and get them to check all flights for Limpy's name," Mario said, "and send them a copy of his photograph and get them to check their security cameras." Pete was on it, he knew the appropriate phone number off the top of his head, he didn't have to look it up. By the time he had made his call and sent Limpy's photograph all four of them were ready to leave and they began to make their way to the squad car.

Forty minutes later they arrived at the floor of the car park where Limpy's car had been found. The entire car park had been cordoned off, so they parked their car at the entrance and they were directed to the floor where Limpy's car was parked by a street cop. It was a cold December day and although the sun was shining, not too much daylight was peering through the confines of the car park by the time they arrived on the floor where Limpy's car was parked. A cold breeze blew through the open floor, although it always seemed to Mario that no matter what the weather was like, it always appeared to be windy at LaGuardia, or at least, any flight he had ever been on involving this airport had always been a turbulent one. There was enough light to see that Chuck's team had already arrived and a couple of them were in the process of rolling a motorized robot from a trailer. Another team was building a wall of sandbags at the edge of the floor that overlooked the Atlantic ocean. Even before all the sandbags were in place, one of the team members went behind the half-built wall and using a remote with a joystick, expertly directed the robot to the rear of Limpy's car.

"Wouldn't want to take that guy on playing a computer game!" Pete whispered to Darlene, tilting his head towards the robot's operator.

Once Chuck's team had completed the wall of sandbags they directed Mario's team to an area behind the sandbags where Chuck and the remote operator were already positioned, sitting in small, canvas, fold-up chairs. The operator began to peer through a periscope that had been placed on a stand as the others were instructed to duck down below the top of the sandbags. The operator then began to consult a video screen that was displaying what the robot was seeing from a camera located on the top of it.

"In position, preparing to unlock the trunk," the operator said. This was a cue for Chuck to stand and give the command to evacuate the floor.

"Clear the area!" Chuck bellowed out through a bullhorn. After a few seconds, he repeated the command, "clear the area!" Chuck then did a visual check looking for anyone in the vicinity, satisfied the rest of the floor was clear, he returned to his seated position. The operator waited a few seconds to allow any unseen stragglers to clear the area then pressed a few buttons on his console. The operator was now looking at a video screen showing a metallic arm beginning to extend from the robot. At the end of the arm was a key which they all assumed must be some sort of master key. The robot flicked the car's logo away from the lock it was concealing, and the key was inserted and turned. There was an audible click as the back hatch clicked open. The arm holding the key then retracted and the robot was moved a few feet to one side. A thinner arm began to move forward from the robot and penetrated the small gap at the side of the vehicle between the hatch cover and the car. There was a camera at the end of this arm and the operator was focused on checking for any form of explosive devices. Satisfied there were none in the back of the car he meticulously maneuvered the robot to search underneath the car and in the engine compartment. Finally, he unlocked the driver's door, manipulated the robot's prosthetics to open the door enough to thread the camera into the interior of the car and after a minute or so he turned to Chuck.

"The car appears to be free of explosives, but I believe there is a body in the trunk of the car!"

Thursday 20th December 2018

Chapter 23

Chuck, not satisfied with just the robot's assessment of the car, now stood and used a hand gesture to two of his men who, unbeknownst to Mario's team, had been patiently waiting in a stairwell. They were heavily dressed in anti-bomb protective gear and they began to move towards the vehicle to provide a further evaluation. Slowly, the two men began walking towards the car. At first, Darlene thought that their almost imperceptible movements were of a cautionary nature until she realized that they couldn't walk any faster in their get-up, even if they wanted to.

"Don't you trust the robot Chuck?" Pete asked.

"Normally, I wouldn't have a problem but if this car belongs to the same person who detonated the cannon on Sunday, I'm not taking any chances," Chuck replied with some concern, "and anyway, it's good training for the guys in a real situation."

It seemed to take an inordinate amount of time for the two men to reach the vehicle and then systematically probe and prod at the exterior and interior of the car. By the time they had finished, all four doors and the hood of the vehicle were open together with the trunk that had been unlatched by the robot. They gave a cursory look at what was in the trunk of the car then provided the all-clear signal to Chuck.

Once Chuck gave Mario, Pete and Darlene the all-clear they immediately sprinted to the back of the vehicle as the two members of Chuck's team began to remove their headgear. The hair on the heads of the two bomb disposal operatives was matted to their foreheads and their faces were red with the effort and strain of working in their cumbersome, protective suits. Other members of Chuck's team rushed forward providing copious amounts of water and assisting the two bomb-disposal experts in extricating themselves from their armor.

Humph labored towards the vehicle using his cane and by the time he approached, it had been confirmed that the body in the back of the car was indeed Shorty. Humph took one look at the prostrate body and the unusual positioning of the victim's head and gave his assessment. "I can't confirm until we carry out a proper post-mortem, but I believe I can say with some certainty that this poor fellow's neck was broken and with some efficiency, I might add," Humph said, almost apologetically.

"Confirming that the killer had received some training in hand-to-hand fighting, suggesting that it may be a military man," Pete said.

"And Limpy was a military man," Darlene said aloud, to no one in particular.

“O.K. Darlene, get Harry’s team over here and we’ll go back to the Gardens,” Mario said, “although I’m not looking forward to telling Gwendoline the news, not looking forward to it one bit.”

Thursday 20th December 2018

Chapter 24

On their return drive to the Gardens, Pete offered to break the news to Gwendoline.

"You may be a little too close to Gwendoline right now and I have had a bit more experience in dealing with this type of event," Pete said.

"No, it's my job," Mario replied, "but what you can do is explain the situation to the rest of the troupe, they may still be searching for Shorty."

"Fair enough," Pete said and not much else was said until they arrived outside Gwendoline's trailer. A few of the performers were still hanging around the trailer and they greeted the foursome with great expectations, hoping for good news. Then they saw the dour looks on the police team's faces and knew that the news was not good. Mario gave a quick rap on Gwendoline's door and without waiting for a reply went into the trailer, closing the door behind him. Pete stepped onto the steps and began to address the circus performers while Darlene and Humph stood beside the trailer.

"As you know, both Limpy and Shorty have been missing since last night," Pete paused as some of the performers were translating his address to others. "We have located Limpy's vehicle and although there is no trace of Limpy, I'm afraid we found Shorty's body in the back of the car." Again, Pete paused as the translations continued amid the anguished cries and tears of the performers. Other performers began to rush over to hear the news and it wasn't long before the entire troupe was gathered outside Gwendoline's trailer.

"I know this is a bad time," Pete continued above the din of the performers, "but if you have any information you could share with us regarding the movements of Limpy or Shorty yesterday evening, no matter how trivial you might think it is, please come forward." But nobody did. Most of the performers were from countries where the police and government authorities were not to be trusted.

Inside Gwendoline's trailer, predictably, the news had not gone down well.

"This is all my fault," Gwendoline wailed, "I should never have hired that terrible man."

"You weren't to know that, Gwen," Mario said in an attempt to console her.

"I should have realized, I should have carried out better background checks," Gwendoline offered.

"But you did, you contacted his previous circus, the person provided you with great credentials. There's nothing more that you could have done," Mario said. "Look, there must have been something between Limpy and Petr, that's the key, and you couldn't possibly have foreseen that! Then, somehow, we don't know how yet, but Shorty got involved. It's not your fault Gwen."

"You may be right Mario, but it still doesn't help," Gwendoline replied as she dabbed more tears from her reddened cheeks. "Do you mind if I remain alone this evening? Under the circumstances, I don't think I'm going to be good company."

"Will you be O.K. on your own?" Mario replied somewhat concerned and wary about leaving her alone in such a depressed state.

"Yes, of course, I'll probably sleep here in the trailer this evening, mourn with the others. I'm sure there will be others out there who will need a shoulder," she indicated with a sideways tilt of her head. "Some of them will need more support than me, Shorty was quite the character."

With no more to be said, Mario left the trailer to join the rest of his team outside.

"So, what's next boss?" Pete asked.

"I was hoping you could tell me, Pete," a confused Mario replied, as he ran a hand through his hair.

"Well, so far we haven't received word of any hits on flights for this guy's name and airport security hasn't spotted him on any of their cameras' feeds," Pete replied dejectedly, "so, indeed, what is next?"

Friday 21st December 2018

Chapter 25

The previous afternoon they had experienced a traumatic few hours finding Shorty's body so Mario had decided to call it a day and told his team to meet at the office early the following morning. That evening Humph would be busy at his lab. performing the autopsy on Shorty, of course, Darlene would be in attendance as his driver. Mario knew that Pete would be home with his family but constantly thinking about the next steps in the investigation, as would he.

So it was that at 7:00 the next morning the team was together, complete with coffees and donuts ready to brainstorm the investigation.

"What did you learn from the autopsy, Humph?" Mario asked, kicking off the meeting.

"As expected, the cause of Shorty's death was a broken neck," Humph replied sadly, "he wouldn't have known anything about it. No sign of a struggle, nothing under the fingernails so that would suggest the murder was carried out quickly and professionally, which ties in with the suspect's military background."

"Pete, any more news from airport security?" Mario asked.

"Nada," Pete replied, "our suspect seemed to have disappeared off the face of the earth. Of course, he could be using a false passport so the name we are looking for won't show up anywhere and he could be clever enough to avoid the cameras or use a disguise."

"So, the killer could have used the airport car-park as a ruse," Darlene suggested. "Maybe he had no intention of catching a flight, he was just using the location to throw us off the scent of his true whereabouts."

"It's possible," Mario replied, "but with his car parked, the only way he could have left LaGuardia, if he was traveling by land, would have been by taxi, bus or by renting a car. Darlene, get a copy of Limpy's photo to the taxi and bus companies to see if any of their drivers remember picking him up at some time yesterday morning. Pete, check with security at the airport to troll the rental car companies."

"On it, boss," Darlene replied. She returned to her desk to start working on the assignment while Pete picked up the phone to pass on new instructions to the LaGuardia security team.

"After you've done that Darlene why don't you and Humph start going through all the photos from both the newspaper guy and Harry's team to see if anything jumps out at you?" Mario quickly added.

"What will we be looking for?" Humph asked, arms outstretched in confusion, not used to being on this side of a police investigation.

"Don't worry Humph," Darlene shouted out, "you'll know when you see it."

“She learns fast,” Pete said, smiling at Mario and tilting his head towards Darlene. Then he added, “so, what will we be doing boss?”

“There’s a large Bosnian community in Queens,” Mario replied, “I thought we could take a drive to the old neighborhood and check out a few of the bars and restaurants to see if anyone has seen the man lately.”

“They’re a pretty tight-knit group, they might not be prepared to discuss anything with the police,” Pete said.

“Yeah, but I’m from Queens, don’t worry about it,” Mario jokingly replied.

Friday 21st December 2018

Chapter 26

Mario and Pete left the others to their assignments as they took the elevator down to the car compound.

"Where are we going to start?" Pete asked, bowing to his boss's appreciation of the area.

"I think we'll start in the Jamaica neighborhood," Mario replied, "check out a few of the bars and restaurants and see where that leads us.

"Great, bureks for lunch!" Pete said with some relish.

"Bureks? What the hell are they?" Mario asked.

"You're from Queens and you don't know what a burek is?" Pete replied with a surprised look on his face.

"I led a very sheltered life growing up," Mario replied.

"It's like a phyllo pastry filled with just about anything but generally meat, cheese, or whatever. It's delicious. I just can't believe you've lived in Queens all your life and you don't know what a burek is? That's amazing," Pete said, continuing to shake his head in surprise at the lack of Mario's unadventurous palate.

"How do you know this shit Pete," Mario asked.

"In fairness, I do have a bit of an advantage on you," Pete confessed.

"You do? What's that then?" Mario was now curious.

"Well, you've met my dad, right?" Pete asked.

"Yes, but he's Italian, not Bosnian!" Mario stated.

"You're right, but he's from Trieste," Pete replied. "We had a family trip there once, beautiful place."

"So, what's the significance of Trieste?" Mario asked.

"Well, Trieste only became part of Italy after the first world war, prior to that it was part of the Austro-Hungarian empire and there was a large Slovenian population living there," Pete explained. "Dad's heritage is Slovenian and bureks are a popular food item there." They had then reached Mario's squad car and he looked across at his partner as he began to get in the passenger's seat.

"Back up the truck a minute!" Mario suddenly said, "if your dad was from Slovenian stock, how come you have a name like Cannatelli?"

"Well, my grandfather changed his name to be more Italian," Pete explained.

"I see, but how did you know you could buy bureks in Queens?" Mario asked.

"One of my first cases was a murder in the South Jamaica area, quelle surprise, that's when I discovered bureks could be bought around this neighborhood," Pete replied.

"Why do you say 'quelle surprise? I'll have you know that Queens is one of the safest boroughs in New York City," Mario chided Pete as he drove out of the compound and headed towards Queens.

"Yeah, but you're from Forest Hills, not South Jamaica!" Pete goaded his boss.

"True, so, change of plan, we will start in the middle of Queens, at Astoria, I know there are a few Bosnian establishments along there," Mario stated.

"Sounds good to me," Pete replied.

The streets of Astoria were bustling with shoppers as tomorrow would be the last weekend of shopping before Christmas.

"That reminds me, I still have to buy presents for my parents," Mario said rhetorically. "I must do that this weekend."

"I don't have to worry about that, fortunately, Marie buys all the presents for everyone and the food for Christmas," Pete said casually.

"Yeah, but don't you have to buy something for Marie?" Mario asked.

"Sure I do," Pete replied, then a thought sprang to him. "Hey, maybe we could get Darlene to buy the presents for us. Bet she would do a better job of it than we could do!"

"Boy, you're pushing it," Mario said laughing, "can I watch while you ask her?" Before Pete could answer, Mario found an available parking spot and pulled in. Just in case, he placed a 'POLICE ON CALL' sign on the dashboard before they left the car.

It was a sunny day, albeit a cold one, as they began to carry out some old-fashioned police work interviewing people in various bars and restaurants. By 1:30, after zero response to the photograph they had been showing people, they decided to have lunch in an appropriately named restaurant called, 'Taste of Bosnia'. There was a bar inside with a row of tall chairs, a couple of them were occupied with what looked like regulars. The main dining area had a few tables and chairs at the front of the restaurant and a line of bench seats at the side, on the way to the kitchen. The place was old and not exactly decorated in a modern style but it was clean and the smells from the kitchen were enticing. The restaurant was about half full and they managed to procure one of the bench seats that afforded them some privacy. When the waiter arrived, Pete ordered a burek along with a beer called Sarajevska, a pale lager, that was imported from Bosnia. Mario ordered the same meal but passed on the beer. It didn't take long for their meal to be served and Mario was impressed with the taste of the food. During the meal, they discussed their next steps but they were a little stumped as to what exactly those next steps were to be. When they received the bill, Mario showed a photograph of the man they were looking for to the proprietor of the restaurant. He politely shook his head as the proprieter revealed no recognition to the photograph. But just at that moment, an older man was walking by carrying in a box of what looked like groceries.

The delivery man was forced to turn sideways to walk past the owner of the establishment as he was holding the photograph. In doing so, he took a quick glance at the picture and instinctively said, “that’s Ahmed!”

Friday 21st December 2018

Chapter 27

"You know this man?" Mario said instantly, his interest immediately piqued.

"Sure, he's been to my store a few times," the man replied with a heavy east European accent. "Look, wait a minute, this box is heavy, I just need to deliver it to the kitchen." The man continued walking down the narrow aisle to a swing door that led into the kitchen. Mario paid the bill and they waited patiently for the old man to return. Eventually, the man came back and stood by the table where Mario and Pete were seated.

"Sorry about the wait, always have to explain what I brought to the chef. I don't know why that should be, it's the same dinner order every day! So why are you looking for Ahmed?" The old man asked with a big smile on his face.

"We're police officers," Mario said as he displayed his badge to the man. It's regarding the death that occurred at the Gardens last weekend."

"Oh, the human cannonball, yeah I read about that," the old man replied, becoming a little more serious now. "So what does that have to do with Ahmed? Apart from the fact that he worked at the circus."

"How well do you know Ahmed?" Mario asked.

"I don't really know him," the old man replied. "He just made infrequent visits to my store to buy a few items to give him a taste of the old country. He always used to stock up on bureks when he was in town. Needless to say, we used to talk about the old days, but I don't really know him."

"You sold him bureks?" Pete asked, as if that was a surprise, especially with all the restaurants in the area.

"Yes, I sold him bureks," the old man said, taken aback a little, then he thought of something, "did you have bureks for your lunch?" The old man asked mischievously.

"Yes, we both did," Pete said and Mario nodded in agreement.

"Then you ate my bureks," the old man replied proudly. "Most of the eateries around here come to me for my baked goods. They're the best."

"Tell me, when was the last time you spoke to Ahmed?" Mario asked.

"Oh, let me think," the old man said and looked down thoughtfully as he toyed with his bottom lip using his forefingers. "It would have been early last Saturday morning, yes that's right. He said they had finished setting up the circus equipment, he had a little time between rehearsals and their first show Saturday afternoon. He told me that he may not be able to come back to see me again during this trip, so he purchased quite a few things."

"You're sure about that? Saturday morning," Pete asked.

"Yes, quite sure," the old man replied.

"Well thank you, Mr.?" Mario asked.

"Kovacevic, Davud Kovacevic," the old man replied, "here's my card, just in case you need some more bureks, I can have them delivered to you."

"Well, thank you very much for your assistance Mr. Kovacevic," Mario said, taking the card. "You've been a great help." With that, the old man bid farewell, walked to the front of the restaurant and left.

"So," Mario said.

"We hit lucky there, but I think walking into any more bars and possibly even restaurants looking for this Ahmed fellow is going to prove fruitless," Pete said.

"You've got that right," Mario replied in a bit of a huff.

"No, it has just occurred to me, our Limpy could be a Bosnian Muslim, so no one would have seen him in bars. Muslims don't drink." Pete said. "I'm thinking, where's the nearest Mosque?" Mario didn't know the answer to that, so he called over to the owner once more and asked him.

"That would be the Bosnian Herzegovinian Islamic Center over on 91st," the man replied, "but be careful, that Jamaica is not a safe area."

"Thanks, we will," Mario replied, and they left the restaurant.

Fifteen minutes later they were parked outside the Mosque.

Friday 21st December 2018

Chapter 28

Mario and Pete walked through the front door of the Mosque into a foyer where there were racks for storing shoes. Pete immediately removed his shoes and placed them on one of the racks. Mario followed his example.

"There will probably be people praying in here," Pete whispered and pointed to the door, "so be quiet, I'm pretty sure someone will come over to us wondering what we're doing here." Mario merely nodded. Pete opened the door to the main hall and prayer room and quietly stepped through. Mario followed and closed the door behind them. Mario had barely closed the door when they were spotted by an elderly man with a wizened, grey beard, dressed all in black and wore a hat that looked more like a turban. The man began to quickly walk towards them with a suspicious look on his face. A couple of other men in the large room also appeared concerned and began approaching Mario and Pete, flanking either side of the elder man. As the elder man neared, he bowed his head in welcome, but his eyes stayed focused on them.

"Selam-alejkum," the man said quietly.

"Selam-alejkum," Pete replied, much to Mario's surprise.

"Kako si?" the man answered but this time it was beyond Pete's repertoire and he said nothing. Sensing that neither of the men in front of him could speak Bosnian, the man resorted to English.

"How can I help you?" The man asked, while the two large men standing either side of him were beginning to look a little agitated and Mario thought they were preparing to show them the door in no uncertain fashion.

"Sir, we are police officers and we were wondering if anyone who attends this mosque knows this man," Pete replied as he flashed his badge and showed the man their picture of Limpy. Mario detected a look of recognition in the man's eyes.

"Please follow me," the man smiled and beckoned them to a door that sported a nameplate that read 'Imam Marković'. As he turned to walk towards the door he dismissed his two henchmen with a simple wave of his hand.

The three of them entered the small office, it was littered with papers and every area of the walls was covered with bookshelves full of books. It spoke to Pete as organized chaos, although he felt certain this man could pinpoint what he was looking for in seconds.

"I don't recall seeing the man here, but then we have many strangers briefly attend here. I would have to make copies of your photograph and distribute it amongst the congregation and hope someone will recognize the man," the old man replied, his accent now very pronounced. He was obviously being protective of his flock which was to be expected. "Imam Marković, that is your name isn't it?" Mario asked. The man merely tilted his head in an apologetic agreement. "Look, we are conducting a murder investigation, two murders in fact, and we have reason to believe, that the man in this photograph is behind the murders." Mario pointed to the photograph of Limpy with some vehemence as he spoke to the Imam, much to the surprise of Pete who had never heard Mario as aggressive as this during an investigation. The Imam shook his head and began to smile.

"No, no, no, that is impossible. Ahmed would never hurt anyone, he is such a gentle soul," the Imam replied.

"But he spent time as an army officer, he would have been expected to kill during his tenure in the military," Pete stated gently.

"He broke codes for the military. Sure, he had been trained to use a gun but that was different, that was war. He never served on the front line, he never killed anyone during the war, why would he murder in civilian life?" the Imam insisted. "His wife and three children had been murdered during that terrible war, he was through with any killing."

"Well, we have overwhelming evidence that says different," Mario said officiously. "When was the last time you saw him?"

"Saturday, he came by for a prayer and he told me he would stop by one more time before heading south for the winter," the Imam recalled.

"Ahmed has gone missing; his car was found at the airport with a body in the trunk," Pete stated and he paused while the Imam absorbed that information. "Do you have any idea where he could be hiding?" Pete asked, still trying to maintain the good cop persona. The Imam merely shook his head and a look of sadness came over him.

"I find it difficult to believe he is hiding from anyone! Ahmed used to perform here for the children between circus runs. People in the community would provide accommodations for him. He was much loved, I can't believe what you are telling me," the Imam whispered. Then a kind of a guilty look flashed across his face, something that didn't go unnoticed by the two detectives and he began to become edgy and fidgety.

"So, you have no idea where he could be going?" Mario asked the question again.

"No, as I mentioned, he told me he would be going to Florida when the circus wrapped up, that's where I assumed, he was going, that's all I know," the Imam said.

"I think you may have an idea where he could be, Imam Marković," Mario said with an ominous overtone. "Do you want us to close this place down while we interrogate every worshipper who attends here?" Mario asked before continuing with his aggressive tone, "we could claim this is a haven for terrorists. Is that what you want?" The Imam put his hands up.

"Alright," the Imam said, then placing the palms of his hands on his desk and attempting to calm himself. "His brother-in-law lives nearby," the Imam paused, attempting to gather his thoughts. "You have to know that Darius, the brother-in-law, is a little, how should I say, mentally challenged. He escaped the massacre that killed his sister, his niece and two nephews. That would be Ahmed's wife and family. But the fact that he had escaped and his sister and family hadn't, has seriously affected him. He is not the only one that has been affected I might add and because of that distressing event, the poor man has never been quite the same. He has receded into a shell and his trust in people, especially those in authority, is almost non-existent. Darius lives with a family in a kind of half-way house and Ahmed would often come and visit. But there is no way Ahmed could be hiding there, no way."

"We will need to go there and talk to this Darius," Pete said.

"I will arrange it if I have to, but I doubt you will get much information from him. He is like dealing with a shy, introverted child," the Imam explained. "Would you mind if I also attended the meeting? It may help calm him."

"I'm sorry, but I will have to insist on questioning him, but I have no problem with you attending the interview, as long as you remain silent and don't interfere," Mario said. "He could be the key to finding Ahmed." The Imam looked up at Mario, clearly not comfortable with the situation he was in. Pete tried to diffuse the situation one more time.

"You may well have been one of the last people to have seen Ahmed before he disappeared. Can you recall what he was wearing?" Pete asked.

"Let me think," the Imam said and closed his eyes to try and think back to the previous Saturday, "a hat, you know, one of those with the ear flaps that can be joined on the top of your head or to cover your ears, a black one I think with grey fur. He wore boots and a thick, blue parka as I recall."

"Thank you," Pete said.

Mario and Pete had exhausted their line of questioning and after exchanging telephone numbers, they thanked the Imam and left his office. They retrieved their shoes from the foyer and returned to their car.

"What do you think?" Pete asked.

"The Imam is convinced he's innocent," Mario said.

"Well, that doesn't mean much. How often have we heard that before about a suspect?" Pete offered.

“You know, let’s just swing by the Gardens and check out Limpy’s trailer. We have made a thorough search of Petr’s trailer but has anyone checked out Limpy’s place?” Mario asked.

“Not to my knowledge,” Pete replied, “but what do you hope to find?”

“Bureks for a start!” Mario replied.

Friday 21st December 2018

Chapter 29

It was mid-afternoon by the time Mario and Pete arrived back at the Garden's compound and they were met by a surprising sight. All the trucks and trailers that carry the circus equipment were now mobilized and ready to leave for their trip down south to Florida. Gwendoline was talking to a few of the fleet's drivers as Mario walked towards her. She was dressed in tight jeans, a red one-piece hoody with the circus's logo on the back and the word 'RINGMASTER' stenciled in a semi-circle across the top, clearly indicating that she was in charge. Although the word was partially obscured by her pony-tail poking through the back of her baseball hat. Mario waited until she had finished giving the drivers their instructions and she turned to greet the two detectives. Mario thought she looked tired and depressed as if all her joie de vivre had been sucked from her with what had happened during the last few days.

"Hi," she said with an attempt at a smile, "I'm glad you showed up, it won't be long before this lot is hitting the road."

"I didn't know you were leaving so soon," Mario replied, "otherwise I would have arrived sooner."

"Well, we needed to move this ensemble out of here, Don't worry, I'm not leaving just yet," Gwendoline explained, "just in case I'm still a suspect." She looked over at Mario with a mischievous smile.

"There aren't as many vehicles as I thought there would be," Mario said looking around at all the trucks, each one adorned with the name of the circus, 'Baxter Family Circus'.

"Well, because of our unpredictable winters, we schedule our last few venues of the tour in arenas like this one," Gwendoline explained, pointing to the Garden's building, "so all the trucks carrying the big top and such returned to Florida a few weeks ago."

"I see, so, if you are not returning to Florida for a few days, you're cutting it fine if you want to drive down by Christmas, aren't you?" Mario asked.

"Actually, now that I am not taking any passengers, I've decided to fly home. I have a flight booked for early Sunday morning so my car has been loaded onto one of the trailers," Gwendoline explained.

"I see, but if you're leaving later, who's going to be taking charge of this convoy?" Mario asked.

"Oh, that would be Jerry. He's the foreman in charge of all the equipment and logistics," Gwendoline answered, pointing to a well-built man dressed in only a Baxter Family Circus t-shirt, jeans and work boots despite the cold. Pete looked over to the man who could easily pass as a bodybuilder then looked back at Mario, he got Pete's drift.

"Did Jerry have anything to do with the truck housing the cannon by any chance?" Mario asked Gwendoline.

"He may have driven it into position in the arena, but other - hey, wait a minute, you can't possibly think that Jerry had something to do with the explosion. Seriously?" Gwendoline asked with her hands on her hips looking offended by the affront to her top guy.

"Well, we were under the impression that only you, Petr and Anton were the only ones that had access to the cannon area," Pete said.

"Well, forgive me," Gwendoline replied with a hint of sarcasm in her voice, "during the circus performances, yes, that's true, but hell, we have to set up. That was neither Petr nor Anton's job. That responsibility fell to Jerry and me."

"So, Jerry nor anybody else would have gone near the cannon after set up?" Pete asked gently, playing good cop again.

"No, in fact, after we had set-up, Jerry was taking a few days off, he's originally from New York but as soon as he heard about the accident he was right back here. One of my best workers, I'd trust him with my life." Gwendoline was adamant and the torrent of words was delivered with an anger that Mario had not seen in the short time he had known her. Gwendoline realized this and instantly calmed.

"By the way, I tried calling you this morning to tell you we were moving the circus out. Of course, you weren't there so I talked to Humph. Which was just as well because we wanted Shorty's body transported to Florida. Humph agreed to release Shorty's body and he kindly arranged a burial transit permit, contacted funeral homes who in turn contacted airlines to transport his remains. We will have a formal burial in Florida. I think Shorty would have wanted that," Gwendoline said with a croaky voice as a small tear trickled down her cheek.

"Quite right," Mario replied, not quite knowing what to say. He had now witnessed another facet in the spectrum of Gwendoline's emotions. There was a small pause in the conversation that was filled by Pete.

"Gwendoline, I know the timing might be inconvenient, under the circumstances," Pete said with a sympathetic tone as he indicated the line of trucks, "but we really do need to carry out a quick search of Limpy's trailer. New evidence has come to light that we need to investigate further and we think we may find some answers in Limpy's trailer."

"Sure, sure thing," Gwendoline replied as she rattled through a ring of keys attached to her belt by a carabiner clip hook. Even though the keys were not marked, she expertly located the one for Limpy's trailer amongst the dozens she was sorting through and handed it to

Pete. "It's been moved since you were last here, it is now hooked up for our trip, it's just over there," Gwendoline pointed to the trailer. Pete started to head towards Limpy's trailer when he heard Mario call out to him.

"I'll catch you up," Mario said.

The step to enter the trailer was now fixed to its traveling position so after unlocking and opening the door, Pete had to make a big step to gain access to the mobile home. The first thing he noticed was Limpy's clown uniform strewn across the floor of the trailer. This appeared to be at odds with the neatness of everything else, as you would expect from an ex-military officer. There was nothing to indicate Shorty had been here. If, as Humph had said, his neck had been broken then there would not necessarily be any blood or signs of a struggle. If there was any of Shorty's DNA around it would prove nothing as Shorty had often been seen coming into Limpy's trailer in the few days before the performances, probably to discuss the act.

Pete moved to the kitchen area, treading carefully to avoid the clown uniform on the floor. There was a small refrigerator with an even smaller freezer section. Pete opened the freezer door and saw there a white plastic bag with the name 'Kovacevic' printed on it. Pete gently opened the bag and inside was a number of bureks amongst some other delectable-looking goodies that even he didn't recognize. With the power source unhooked from the trailer in preparation for the trip, the bag's contents had already defrosted. He made a mental note to pay another visit to Davud Kovacevic at some point in the near future. He would love to discover more about other examples of Bosnian cuisine.

After closing the freezer door, he walked over to the closet. He was just opening the door when Mario entered the trailer, having finished his extra-curricula conversation with Gwendoline.

"Anything?" Mario asked.

"Oh yes," Pete replied, "I'm beginning to have real problems with these two murders!"

"How so?" Mario asked.

"You're right, the bureks are over there in the freezer, Pete said as he sat down on the bed that was near the closet he was looking through. "Now why, after going to all the trouble to travel to Astoria to buy those pastries, knowing that he would be leaving, would he leave them behind?"

"Left in a hurry maybe. The murder of someone can cloud your judgment," Mario replied in a feeble attempt to offer an explanation. But Mario wasn't giving it a great deal of thought, he was too busy studying the contents of the trailer. One of the objects that caught his eye was the replica clown's egg Gwendoline had told him about during dinner. The egg was painted with Limpy's face and enclosed in a protective glass case. But Pete was not to be dissuaded, he continued with his line of thought.

"O.K. then master sleuth, here's an overcoat," Pete said, pulling out the bottom of the coat from the closet to show Mario.

"An overcoat?" Mario asked, confusion written all over his face.

"An overcoat," Pete replied, letting go of the coat's hem.

"And, the significance of that is?" Mario asked.

"It's winter, it's cold. Why would he leave without his hat, gloves, boots and overcoat?" Pete asked. Mario looked inside the closet to see the hat and coat, exactly as the Imam had described them.

"So, there could be a million explanations as to why he left them behind. What problem do you have specifically?" Mario asked.

"Well, here we have an alleged murderer of two people and he has high-tailed it to who knows where with no cold-weather clothing. Then, in another trailer, we have someone who has been murdered for whom we could not find any cold-weather clothing. It's not making any sense!" Pete said.

Friday 21st December 2018

Chapter 30

"Simple," Mario replied, "the Great Grando's coat was better than Limpy's. From the descriptions we've received of the two men and after looking at photographs of them, they're not much different in size." Before anymore discussion could be had, there was a knock on the open trailer door.

"Hey guys, are you just about done in here? We're ready to haul arse," one of the truck drivers asked them. He didn't ask it so much in the form of a question but more of a request.

"Yeah, we'll get out of your hair," Mario said, and Pete rose from the bed and began gathering up not only Limpy's strewn clown outfit but also a laundry bag of soiled clothing. Mario wasn't quite sure why Pete was retrieving the costume, so he questioned it.

"O.K., I give up. Why do we need these items?" Mario asked.

"This trailer is on its way down south and when it arrives at its destination it's going to be cleaned out. I just have a feeling in my gut that we might be needing these clothes," Pete said.

"You have a feeling!" Mario said sarcastically.

"Yes, I do. Something is not quite right about this case and we may need DNA to unravel it," Pete replied.

"Unravel what, specifically?" Mario asked in frustration.

"I don't know yet," Pete replied, equally frustrated.

“Are you sure we don’t need anything else, the light fixtures perhaps?” Mario continued, striking up his sarcastic tone again.
“Good thinking, I’ll also grab the bureks. They’re going to be inedible by the time they arrive in Florida. I can eat some of those on the way back to the office.” Pete told Mario. Despite what Mario had said to Pete, he gently picked up the clown’s egg representing Limpy’s unique features and took that with him. During the trip to Florida, the unsecured egg could end up in a broken heap on the floor of the trailer and Mario didn’t think that should happen to something so reverent.

Pete left the trailer with the clothes and Mario had the bag of bureks as they went to find Gwendoline to return the trailer key to her. They saw her standing in the middle of the compound organizing the convoy. She reminded Mario of one of those wagon masters he used to see on TV when he watched old western series. Mario walked over to her and handed her the key while Pete walked over to their car and placed the items retrieved from Limpy’s trailer on the back seat. Mario had a few more words with Gwendoline, they embraced, then he joined Pete at the car. She waved to them as they left the compound ahead of the first of the trucks that were about to leave.

When they arrived back at the office with what was left of the bureks, they were surprised to see that Darlene had been spending her time creating an evidence board containing photographs of the victims, murder suspects, times and dates with ribbons connecting relevant information. Humph was sitting at a desk avidly searching through the photographs.

"Wow Darlene I'm impressed, although I'm not sure Gwen should be tagged as a suspect," Mario said sincerely as he inspected the board.

"You can't say that she shouldn't," Darlene countered.

"Here Darlene, you can hang this costume up beside the board. It might provide us with some inspiration because I sure as hell have none left," Pete said as he dumped the outfit on her desk and placed the bag of laundry in the corner of the office. Darlene began to inspect the costume's material, running her fingers up and down feeling the quality.

"This is silk, this isn't a cheap costume," Darlene said, surprised at the quality of the material. She found a hanger and reverently attached it to a clothes hook on the wall. Just then, a phone rang on Humph's temporary desk, he picked it up as he had been doing all day as Mario's phone had been forwarded to his in Mario's absence. The conversation took only seconds. Humph looked at Mario with some consternation.

"That was Larry at the front desk, Commissioner Harper is on his way up!"

Friday 21st December 2018

Chapter 31

Mario was glad the front desk had extended the same courtesy to Mario of forewarning him about the Commissioner's arrival that they used to do for Chief Horowitz, but he wasn't sure he was ready for Harper right now. He didn't have time to dwell on the problem though, as Commissioner Harper and his entourage of yes-men and yes-women, six in all, stormed into the office. The Commissioner was a tall man, who always stood erect and he held his head high as he walked briskly almost military style. He was always immaculately well-dressed in tailor-made suits, and there was hardly ever a follicle of his well-groomed hair out of place. Clean-shaven and a regular visitor to his manicurist he was always perfectly presentable for the television cameras that could be suddenly thrust in front of him at any moment of the day. He was always prepared. Add to the package his fine Hamptons, Ivy League voice, that sounded so commanding on the television, which was now being directed at Mario.

"Now look here detective, this second murder," the Commissioner was blaring out in his usual obnoxious manner as if the murder had been purposely committed by Mario and his team to slight him. But then he suddenly stopped. He was looking towards the evidence board that Darlene had created, but more specifically at Limpy's discarded costume that was hanging beside the board. He physically paled and began to struggle to get his breath. He immediately turned on his heel and left the room leaving his besotted entourage looking in a confused state, not knowing whether to follow the man or holdfast. Then his voice bellowed out from down the hall.

"I'll catch you later detective, places to be, unfortunately," with those hasty words from the Commissioner the group of yes-people scurried out of the room to catch up with Harper leaving Mario's team looking at each other zombified and speechless. Until Pete burst out laughing.

"What the hell just happened here?" Mario asked with his arms outstretched.

"We now know how to keep old Harper away from here!" Pete said, still laughing.

"I'm sorry what am I missing here?" Mario asked while Humph and Darlene looked on, equally as mystified at the Commissioner's sudden departure and why Pete was so obviously enjoying it.

"Don't you see? Harper took one look at the clown costume and clammed up," Pete explained. "Obviously he suffers from coulrophobia, a fear of clowns. All we have to do is ask your girlfriend Gwen for some posters that feature clowns. I'm sure she will have some. Then we can paste them on the walls, Harper won't set foot in this office again. Mario, you could keep Limpy's egg on your desk and use it as a paperweight. That would act as a deterrent."

"Ha," Humph suddenly blurted out, "yes it certainly fits, well done Pete." Then the others began to laugh.

"Strange name for a phobia," Darlene said.

"Not nearly as strange as hippopotomonstrosesquippedaliophobia," Pete managed to say with some difficulty.

"O.K., got me there," Humph said. "What the hell does that mean? I'm not going to even attempt repeating it!"

"Ironically, it's a fear of long words," Pete replied. "I think some people who compile our vocabularies must have a sense of humor. I mean why is 'abbreviation' such a long word?"

"How do you know this shit, Pete?" Humph asked with a smile. However, the humorous sidebar didn't last long as Pete's phone began to ring, call display revealing the F.B.I. Pete picked up the phone.

"Cannatelli here," Pete said, all serious now.

"Hey Pete, Simmons here. We've finally got a hit on your man Petr Stojanovski from Interpol's facial recognition database but you're not going to like it."

Friday 21st December 2018

Chapter 32

Pete pressed the speakerphone button so the rest of the team could hear the conversation.

"The man identified in the photograph is one Nikola Petrović, a Serbian who is wanted for war crimes, specifically for being one of the protagonists during the Srebrenica massacre in 1995," agent Simmons explained.

"You've got to be kidding me!" Was the best Pete could muster in reply. "Are you certain of this?"

"100% sure. Checked and double-checked. He somehow eluded capture after the troubles in 1995 and disappeared off the face of the earth. Interpol and other agencies have been looking for him for years so it looks like you have done them all a favor. They can strike him off their books," Simmons told him, "and didn't you say you are still looking for the guy in the other photograph you sent?

"Yes, Ahmed Isaković," Pete replied.

"Well, he was Bosnian, right? So, there's your motive!" Simmons offered.

"Apparently, Isaković's family was murdered during that very massacre. Although Isaković wasn't present he would have certainly recognized Petrović from photographs and that's why he must have done murdered him," Pete surmised.

“So, now all you have to do is find this Ahmed fellow,” Simmons said. “Well if you need any help, you know where to find us, we owe you one for bringing this Petrović fellow to our attention.

“No problem,” Pete said but then he thought of something else, “what exactly was Petrović’s trade in the army?”

“Let me see,” Simmons replied. Over the speakerphone the team could hear keys being tapped, “there it is, ordnance, he was in ordnance, if that helps.”

“Sure does, thanks,” Pete replied but a confused look appeared on his face as he bade his farewell to Simmons.

“What’s wrong Pete?” Mario asked. “This is great news, it looks like all the pieces are fitting into place, well apart from Ahmed’s capture that is.” But Pete didn’t appear to be so convinced.

“Fitting into place? I think someone has just kicked the puzzle all over the floor.”

Friday 21st December 2018

Chapter 33

"What do you mean Pete?" Darlene asked, "you're not making any sense."

"Well, that's because this case is not making any sense," Pete said a little more belligerently than was necessary. "On the one hand, we have a kind, gentle individual who was great with children who spent his time in the army as a cipher specialist who we are assuming is the murderer of two men. On the other hand, we have an alleged victim who is a known killer, a war criminal, a murderer and an explosives specialist, precisely the very method used in the first murder. Now does that make any sense to you?"

"Yes, if Limpy recognized the Great Grando as Nikola Petrović the war criminal," Mario countered, "he may have become incensed enough to carry out the murder. And how can you say that the Great Grando is the '***alleged***' victim when we know for a fact that he is the victim; he is the only performer unaccounted for. Humph's DNA findings confirmed it."

"Point of order," Humph chipped in, "I merely confirmed the victim was male and approximately the same age as the alleged victim."

"Precisely. Then there are the bureks and the overcoats," Pete added, "they're bothering me. Something is not right here, it is not adding up."

"Well, until they do add up, damn the bureks and the overcoats, Pete. Until we can come up with a better theory, we are still looking for Limpy, alias Ahmed Isaković," Mario said, now he too was beginning to get a little irate. This was the first time Darlene had witnessed the two detectives raising their voices at each other in anger. She wanted to say something to calm them.

"Bureks?" Darlene asked, wondering whatever the hell they were and what they had to do with the case, "what the hell are they?"

"Limpy had gone to Queens to buy bureks, they're a kind of meat patty, a taste of home. There's a particular store he used to go to and he had told the shopkeeper that it would be his last trip to his shop for a while. But when we searched Limpy's trailer we found the bureks in the freezer. Limpy had gone out of his way to buy them and other goodies, so why would they still be in a freezer in his trailer?" Pete clarified.

Everyone was quiet for a moment or two and Darlene wanted to break the silence but being the relative newbie on the team she didn't think it was her place to do so. Fortunately, it wasn't necessary, as Humph entered the fray with a startling new insight into the investigation.

"Oh my God, that's it!" Humph suddenly said. Everyone looked across at the excited ME. "Guys, I've been diligently looking through all these photographs, as you asked me to do, and what I can tell you is that there's no further point in searching for Ahmed Isaković aka Limpy, you're never going to find him," Humph said as he looked up from the pile of photographs that he had been analyzing that were scattered across his desk.

"Well gee thanks, Humph, it's great to think you have so much confidence in us," Pete said with his usual hint of sarcasm.

"No, Pete, you don't understand," Humph replied, "you're not going to find him because, quite simply, he's already dead!"

Friday 21st December 2018

Chapter 34

Mario, Pete and Darlene turned to look at Humph, each one had a look of incredulity on their faces.

"What the hell do you mean, he's already dead?" Mario asked.

"Precisely that, he's dead," Humph replied. "It was Limpy who was killed in the cannon, not the Great Grando."

"Oh, you're going to have to explain this one to me," Pete said as he sat back in his chair with his arms folded across his chest.

"If you'll permit me," Humph began, "I'm saying that Nikola Petrović killed Limpy then impersonated him, giving the impression that no murder had been committed and after the accident, only the Great Grando appeared to be missing. That's because Petrović had placed Limpy's body in the cannon to be caught up in the fire."

"What?" Mario questioned, "how do you figure that?"

"As you know, Darlene and I have been reviewing all the photographs, both those from Harry and the newspaper guy," Humph began to explain. "In addition, we've each come up with idiosyncrasies that haven't made sense, until now, and I believe my theory will solve all of those too."

"Oh, for Pete's sake, get on with it Humph," Pete wailed as he rose from the seat at his desk and walked over to Humph's.

“I’m getting there, Pete, be patient,” Humph reprimanded the detective. “First of all, take a look at this photograph taken by the newspaperman during Saturday’s performance.” The other two detectives joined Pete and they all huddled around Humph’s desk. Humph showed the trio a picture of Shorty standing next to Limpy. “Note how tall Shorty is against Limpy in this photograph. Now, look at this one, taken on Sunday, just before the accident.” Humph displayed another photograph of the two performers. “You notice that in the first photograph the peak of Shorty’s hat is positioned at Limpy’s armpit but in the Sunday’s photograph it is a good two inches shorter.”

“And, the significance of that is?” Pete asked.

“It’s because in the first photograph Limpy was Ahmed Isaković but in this second photograph it was the Great Grando, alias Petr or Nikola, dressed in Limpy’s costume just before he cut out to don his Great Grando uniform,” Humph said.

“It could simply be the jaunt of Shorty’s hat or the angle of the camera,” Mario said, “that proves nothing.”

“Hear me out,” Humph replied, “here’s a photograph of Limpy helping to extinguish the fire.”

“Yes, together with many of the other performers,” Pete said.

“Correct, but look at Limpy’s feet,” Humph said pointing, drawing the team’s attention to them on the photograph, “where are his big, blue, clown’s shoes?”

“Well, wearing them would have been too dangerous in an emergency, plonking down big feet like that during. Removing them would have made sense,” Mario said.

“That’s true, but there are no photographs of Limpy with the big, blue shoes on prior to the fire. But let me give you a theory that would explain all this,” Humph replied excitedly. “What if the Great Grando removed his tunic while he was in the cannon and when the lights went out, he quickly jumped out of the cannon appearing as Limpy the clown? Except, nobody saw him exit the cannon because, as part of the act, all the lights were out.”

“But surely after the accident, one of the performers would have noticed it wasn’t the real Limpy. Even greasepaint wouldn’t have been able to conceal Petr’s features,” Pete stated.

“During the fire, everyone would have been too busy to notice and afterward, unless someone got real close to him you wouldn’t have realized it wasn’t the real Limpy. Why would you? From all accounts, after the accident, the new Limpy either stayed in his trailer or kept his distance,” Humph explained.

“Jeez Humph, I find this a little far-fetched. Maybe you should go back to working at the lab.” Mario suggested.

"No, hear me out," Humph replied adamantly. "Remember we had noticed that when the Great Grando was introduced on Sunday, he didn't remove his helmet," Humph showed photographs of the Great Grando's entrance during the Sunday's performance to remind them. "But during Saturday's performance, he carried the helmet in his hand," Humph said.

"And?" Mario prompted.

"On Sunday he was wearing the makeup of Limpy the clown and underneath his Great Grando suit he was wearing Limpy's costume," Humph answered. "As soon as he climbed into the cannon, out of sight of everyone, he began undressing. He removed his helmet and took off his suit. During the countdown, when the lights went out, he quickly extricated himself from the cannon as Limpy the clown, sans the shoes because those he couldn't put on within the confines of the cannon."

"But the Great Grando's body was found amongst the ashes of the cannon," Darlene said.

"No, ***a*** body was found amongst the ashes of the cannon. Petr, Nikola or the Great Grando, whatever you want to refer to him as, had previously placed the prostrate body of Limpy at the base of the cannon surrounded by explosives and incendiaries. It was the ashes of Limpy we found on the ground, not those of the Great Grando."

"This is a bit of a stretch isn't it Humph?" Mario asked before adding, "a body the size and weight of Limpy would have been difficult to move without anyone seeing it being transported, and then negotiating it into the confined space of the cannon would have been difficult for one man. After all, I know Petr was supposed to be fit but as you said the other day, he was no spring chicken."

"Between them, Petr and Anton transported fireworks backward and forwards all the time, so no one would have given it a thought," Humph countered. "What's more, it checks all the boxes, the wearing of the helmet, the suicide note, and the size differentials in the photographs," Humph said as he looked at the detectives inquiringly. "Furthermore, there's not one photograph that I can find where Limpy and the Great Grando are seen pictured together on the day of the accident but there are numerous photos of them in the same shot taken on the previous day."

"That's possible because during his performance all the performers would have been leaving the arena as the Great Grando was being introduced," Mario suggested, "so there wouldn't be many if any, photographs of them both together, so that proves nothing."

"But Humph's theory would explain my issue with the overcoats," Pete added, beginning to buy into the theory. "The missing one in Petr's trailer and the ones found in Limpy's."

"It would also explain the missing computer and calculations," Darlene chipped in.
"And the bureks," Pete also added, "not to mention Limpy's clown egg that was left on his desk in the trailer. You said yourself Mario you were surprised that he would forget to take that with him if he was leaving? That's a treasured possession to a clown."
"Yes, true, but this is all circumstantial, you still don't have any real proof," Mario added, almost discounting Humph's theory.
"Ah, but I do!" Humph said with a proud grin. "It would also account for why the Great Grando remained dressed as Limpy long after the accident. He couldn't reveal to the other performers that he was, in reality, the Great Grando. He could easily hunch his shoulders a little to feign his height and the limp wouldn't have been difficult to replicate. Under the circumstances, who would have taken much notice? It would also account for why he was on the scene so quickly fighting the fire after the accident."
"Anton was also on the scene quickly, so what? I repeat, everything you have given us so far is circumstantial," Mario said stoically. "You still have butkus."
"But ye of little faith, I have yet to deliver my coup de gras," Humph said as he theatrically placed another photograph on top of all the others that were lying on his desk. "Take a look at this. This is one of Harry's team's photos taken before the truck crunched up all the

evidence. There's the knee-cap I took to the lab.," he pointed to a charred round object before running his finger down the picture a little, "and there, my doubting, dogged detective are the remains of the surgical pins that were used to repair Limpy's injured leg."

Friday 21st December 2018

Chapter 35

Pete returned to his desk and sat slovenly down in his chair, placed his hands together behind his head, and searched the ceiling for inspiration. Mario and Darlene said nothing.

"Well?" Humph asked, looking terribly disappointed that no one was congratulating him on his discovery. "What do you think?" Still, nobody replied. "You see, the surgical pins are made from titanium and some of them survived the fire. Titanium has to be exposed to a really, high temperature for it to burn. I guess the murderer knew that which is why he used so many incendiary bombs because they would do the job if they were juxtapositioned to the body. But, judging by this photograph, obviously, some of the pins avoided destruction." It must have been a good two minutes before anyone spoke and it was Pete.

"I can't see any faults in your theory, Humph," Pete said. "You're right, it does explain just about everything. Well done! Not bad for an old saw-bones." Darlene gave a beaming smile to Humph as a compliment from Pete was a rare thing.

"Hey, less of the ***old,*** and what do you mean, '***just about everything***'?" Humph asked looking deflated because of a potential flaw in his theory.

"Oh no, your theory holds, but it doesn't explain the motive for Shorty's death?" Pete asked.

"The last time anyone saw Shorty was as he was entering Limpy's trailer, right?" Mario said as the cogs were now turning in his brain. "That was the night Limpy or the man we thought was Limpy, said he was leaving for Florida. What if Shorty inadvertently burst in on him just as he was removing his makeup? He would have seen him close up, he would have recognized the Great Grando and the game would have been up."

"So, Nikola would have been forced to silence him," Darlene added.

"That fits," Pete said. "Nikola would have no compunction in doing the deed and with his military training poor Shorty wouldn't have stood a chance."

"If it's any consolation, Gwen will be relieved to hear that Limpy wasn't responsible for Shorty's death after all," Darlene said.

"So, we've been spinning our wheels looking for the wrong guy all along," Mario said dejectedly. "Now we have to start all over again looking for this Nikola guy." Mario began to pace around the room thinking things through. Suddenly he stopped and pointed to Limpy's costume that was hanging on the wall. "Right now, all we have is just a theory but if you're right Humph, and I'm not doubting it for a second, that clown suit should hold two sets of DNA, Limpy's and that of the Great Grando."

"Ha, old Cannatelli nailed it again!" Pete shouted out referring to his gut feel about needing the costume for evidence gathering.

"Yeah yeah," Mario said reluctantly before continuing with instructions, "Darlene, get the costume over to Harry to see what she can come up with."

"They might also need that laundry bag I put in the corner for DNA comparison," Pete chipped in. Darlene looked over at the stray bag and nodded her head.

"Pete, you have to contact airport security again and see if they can spot our new suspect on any of their cameras. Also, put out an APB to all precincts, airports, train and bus stations, the works," Mario told him.

"On it boss but I wouldn't mind betting though, as Darlene suggested when we first thought it was Limpy, that parking at the airport was a ruse to get us to think he has fled the city," Pete replied. "He's obviously got very good at eluding the authorities and he's probably holed up somewhere in the city."

"Do it anyway, meanwhile I'll –" Mario began, just as the phone on Humph's desk rang. It was probably for Mario as his line had remained forwarded to Humph's phone while he was out of the office. He stopped in mid-sentence and reached forward to answer the call.

"Simpson here," Mario said.

"Good afternoon, Detective Simpson, this is Imam Marković," the Imam said very quietly.

"Hi, how's it going?" Mario asked casually.

"Look, I've spoken to Darius, Ahmed's brother-in-law, and I have arranged a meeting with you –" the Imam was cut-off by Mario.

"Imam, my apologies for interrupting you but our investigation has taken a new direction," Mario began, but now it was his turn to be interrupted.

"Does that mean Ahmed is innocent?" The Imam asked.

"Are you going to be at the mosque for the next little while?" Mario asked.

"I will be here for the rest of the day," the Imam replied, now a little concerned, "what has happened?"

"We'll be there as soon as we can to explain," Mario replied and put the phone down. He knew his action was rude but he felt he was about to inadvertently let the cat out of the bag and he didn't want to do that over the phone. Then Mario had another thought.

"By the way Darlene, you will also need to contact to all the taxi and bus companies again, cancel the search for Limpy and get a picture of Nikola Petrović to them to see if anyone will remember picking him up at LaGuardia," Mario instructed.

"Will do," Darlene replied.

Darlene had called Harry, she was sending one of her boys over to pick up the costume, much to Darlene's displeasure. Her thoughts on those guys who worked for Harry were that they were scumbags and she didn't relish the thought of being ogled by them, as they seemed to do every time she encountered them. Right now Darlene couldn't let those thoughts distract her as she began calling the transportation companies. Meanwhile, Pete was contacting airport security to arrange for a scan of their videos with the photograph he was now sending to them. While Pete and Darlene were busy making their calls, Mario decided to return to his office. As a courtesy, Humph removed the call-forwarding. Good timing, as no sooner had he done that, Mario's phone rang. It was the Commissioner.

Friday 21st December 2018

Chapter 36

"Good afternoon Commissioner," Mario said politely.

"Apologies for that swift departure earlier, Simpson," the Commissioner said. "Something came up unexpectedly." I bet it did, thought Mario as the Commissioner continued, "but look here, we now have two murders on our hands. What are you doing about them Simpson?"

"There has been a serious development in the investigation Commissioner," Mario began. "The person of interest is now the Great Grando himself and he is in fact also wanted for war crimes in Bosnia."

"I don't understand, I thought he was the person killed in the accident and he's a war criminal you say?" the Commissioner questioned.

"Yes sir, we now believe that he murdered Limpy, one of the circus clowns and it was his body that was found after the fire. We suspect that the Great Grando also killed the other clown, Shorty was his name, because he had discovered it was the Great Grando posing as Limpy," Mario explained.

"This is all so convoluted, but how is it possible?" The Commissioner asked.

"We have reason to believe that Limpy's body had already been placed in the cannon and after the Great Grando climbed into it during Sunday's performance, he removed his suit and climbed out as Limpy the clown just before the explosion," Mario elucidated.

"My God, the old switcheroo," the Commissioner said. The *'old switcheroo'*? thought Mario. "So, the Great Grando is wanted for war crimes eh? That may well be out of our jurisdiction Simpson," the Commissioner concluded.

"We still have to apprehend the man for two murders Commissioner," Mario said forcefully.

"I understand that, but you may have to hand over what you have to the F.B.I. They have an International Human Rights Unit, let them continue with the investigation. If there is a war criminal in the country they will work with Immigration and Customs Enforcement department, commonly known as ICE. It's out of our hands now," the Commissioner was adamant, "out of interest, what war crimes is the man charged with?"

"His participation in The Srebrenica massacre in Bosnia. The Great Grando's real name is Nikola Petrović and he is Serbian," Mario explained.

"Well, let's leave this one to the powers that be, Simpson. Good timing with Christmas coming, you can have a few well-earned days off," which was the Commissioner's poor attempt at a joke with only four days to go and two of those being a weekend.

"But the powers that be haven't been able to find him sir," Mario offered.

"Well, what makes you think you can find him?" The Commissioner questioned him. Mario was silent for a moment. The Commissioner was right, he had no idea where to begin to look for their killer, he could be anywhere. Probably has numerous ids., false passports and the trail was already getting cold, he could be anywhere by now. He couldn't dwell on the subject too long because the Commissioner was on a roll. "Serbian eh?" The Commissioner mused, "I recall being invited to a fund-raising gala for the St. Sava Cathedral, a Serbian church a couple of years ago. They'd had a devastating four-alarm fire there in 2016 and I was involved at the time because it was suspected arson, after all, they'd previously had a bomb go off there in the sixties. As it turned out, the fire was officially classified as being caused by unextinguished candles that set off the blaze. Met a Bishop somebody or other at the gala, can't remember his name for the life of me. Anyway, he was still living in the Parish House as that had escaped damage during the fire. Nice location though, right there in Manhattan, don't you think?"

"Certainly sir," Mario replied, but he really wasn't listening anymore. A plan of attack was forming in his head and he was trying to think of a way of persuading the Commissioner to let him remain on the case, at least for a few more days.

Friday 21st December 2018

Chapter 37

Mario managed to negotiate an extension to his investigation with the Commissioner. Mario asked for an extra 24 hours before he would be forced to inform the appropriate authorities regarding the identity of their suspect, the war criminal. But Mario felt the Commissioner was feeling a little Christmas spirit and because it was Friday and contacting anyone right before the holidays may be a challenge, he gave Mario until Monday morning to find the Great Grando. If they hadn't located their man by then, all bets were off and the case would be handed over. Mario finished his conversation with the Commissioner and he left his office to go and explain the situation to the others.

"The Commissioner mentioned the large Serbian Cathedral in Manhattan. I know it's a long shot but I would bet that the Bishop there has some ins on where our suspect could possibly be hiding out," Mario said, then continued, "but first, we have to visit the Imam and tell him what has happened to Ahmed then we'll swing by the church and see if we can obtain some information."

"One of us has to remain here to wait for Harry's team to collect the costume and I have to drive Humph to his doctor, so I'll stay here," Darlene explained. "His foot is much better now so he's hoping the doctor will be giving him the go-ahead to be able to drive again."

“Fingers crossed,” Humph said, “although I quite like having a chauffeur.” That remark drew a filthy look from Darlene.

“Well that will be something,” Pete said, “you couldn’t drive before the accident!” Now it was Humph’s turn for a filthy look, directed at Pete for his ribbing.

“Right, why don’t we all meet here first thing in the morning?” Mario said. Everyone groaned as it was the last Saturday before Christmas, but they all reluctantly agreed.

An hour later, Mario and Pete were walking into the Mosque in Queens. They removed their shoes but this time the Imam saw them and immediately gestured them over to his office. He finished up discussing something with one of his followers and then joined the detectives at his office door.

“Come in, come in,” the Imam said politely. When they were all seated, Mario began.

“I’m afraid Imam Marković that I have some bad news for you,” Mario began solemnly. “After further investigation we have discovered that it was Ahmed that was killed in the incident at the circus with the cannon.” A look of disbelief appeared on the Imam’s face.

“That can’t be, you said you were searching for him!” It was spoken barely as a whisper, “and I saw pictures of him in the paper the next day. Ahmed was attempting to put out the fire.”

“We have reason to believe that he was murdered, the body then placed in the cannon by his murderer who then impersonated Ahmed,” Mario explained.

“But who would want to do such a thing? Ahmed was such a gentle, man,” the Imam said. “Why?” He spread his hands out in a futile questioning gesture.

“It appears that the Great Grando was a fugitive, in fact, we think he was a Serbian war criminal. We believe that Ahmed recognized him and he was murdered because of it,” Mario explained. The Imam’s response was to shake his head.

“Will this madness ever end?” The Imam said quietly, still shaking his head in disbelief.

“That’s why there will be no need to trouble Ahmed’s brother-in-law with any questions. We believe it would no longer serve any purpose, we can spare him any further distress,” Mario told the distraught Imam, “but if you would like us to tell him of Ahmed’s death, we could do that.”

“No, no, thank you but this is an unfortunate part of my job. Do you know authorities are still uncovering bodies in mass graves scattered all over our country?” The Imam asked them, “sometimes the bodies are identified, sometimes not. A few are related to worshippers of this mosque, occasionally it falls on me to tell them.”

“I’m sorry,” Mario replied reverently, not knowing quite what to say to the Imam. “Well, we’ll leave you for now,” Mario said as he and Pete rose to leave. “We’re going to the Serbian church in Manhattan now. We’re hoping to obtain ideas as to where to search for Ahmed’s killer.” At that, the Imam gave them a look containing such venom and hate which surprised even Pete.

“They will tell you nothing,” the Imam hissed through clenched teeth. “To this day, some of their leaders are still celebrating the war and what was carried out in the name of war. They will tell you nothing, but I warn you, be careful, be very careful.”

Friday 21st December 2018

Chapter 38

Darlene was just completing some paperwork when one of the guys from Harry's team arrived to collect Limpy's costume. Darlene recognized him as one of the smarmy, photographers that she had seen with Harry during previous cases. He had a camera hanging off a strap around his neck and he was carrying what looked like a shoulder bag for packing suits when you are traveling.

"Hi, I'm David. I don't think we have been officially introduced," the man said as he held out his hand in greeting. Darlene reluctantly accepted his outstretched hand while Humph kept a wary eye on the visitor.

"Detective Darlene Knight," Darlene replied, trying to keep the conversation formal.

"My, so this is it," David said as he walked, uninvited, over to the outfit hanging by Darlene's desk, she, in turn, retreated to where Humph was seated. David gently felt the material and had the same reaction that Darlene had.

"Wow, this stuff isn't cheap!" David remarked.

"No, it's not, so handle it with care," Darlene said, maybe a little too abruptly. "In fact, maybe you shouldn't be touching it at all with your bare hands."

"Don't worry, I'll take good care of it, and anyway, it's the inside of the costume we're going to be testing, not the outside," David replied as he removed the lens cover from his camera and made some adjustments to its settings. "I'll just take a couple of pics before bagging it." He pointed his camera at the costume and began taking photographs from various angles. Darlene looked at Humph and screwed her face up in a 'what the hell is he doing' fashion because, to be honest, Darlene could not think of one good reason why this process was necessary, but she said nothing. After a moment, David turned towards Darlene.

"Darlene, would you mind if I took some photographs with you standing next to the costume please?" David asked.

"No, I don't think so," Darlene replied curtly.

"For perspective, you know size perspective, it might be useful," David preyed on her detective qualities. Reluctantly, Darlene walked slowly over and stood by the hanging costume while David snapped a couple of photos. Then, David asked Darlene to turn sideways, which she did automatically while he continued to take pictures. But when he asked her to move to the other side and face the costume, she became a little suspicious.

"Is this really necessary?" Darlene asked vehemently.

"Sorry, it would be a great help," David replied. Grudgingly, Darlene stepped to the other side. She stood there while David took more pictures but after hearing numerous shutter depressions, she walked back to Humph's desk.

David laid the bag he had brought with him on the floor and began to unzip the sides to open it up. The inside of the bag was lined with thick cellophane, assumingly to protect any evidence, Darlene thought. David then donned some latex gloves before carefully taking the costume off the hanger and gently laying it in the bag. Equally as careful, he deftly flipped one side of the bag towards the other and zipped it back together again.

"Right, that's it then. I'm sure Harry will keep you in the loop on any updates," David said as he rose from the floor bringing the shoulder bag with him. Darlene then remembered to give David the bag of soiled laundry. She walked over to the corner of the office and picked up the bag and handed it to David.

"Apparently it is dirty laundry, Pete told me to give it to you," Darlene said. In turn, he gave a smile that was directed squarely at Darlene, "thank you Darlene for your co-operation." If it wasn't for the fact that David quickly left the office with a parting nod to Humph, Darlene felt her next move was going to be to wipe that lascivious smile off David's face.

Friday 21st December 2018

Chapter 39

Mario drove to the Serbian Cathedral in Manhattan, parked the car and then the two detectives began walking to the Parish House. They arrived at the front door of the house and Mario noticed a doorbell camera security was installed, he rang the bell. After about a minute's wait, the door was opened by someone who was not a butler but who was obviously a man of the cloth. The man opened the door wide but said nothing.

"Good evening," Mario began, "my name is Detective Simpson and this is Detective Cannatelli," Mario showed his NYPD badge to the doorman. "We'd like to speak with the Bishop of the Cathedral, please."

"Which Bishop would that be?" The man replied suspiciously. "We have a few Bishops in attendance this evening."

"The one in charge," Mario replied with some frustration, thinking this guy was a pedantic prick.

"May I tell the Bishop what this is about?" The man asked.

"I'm afraid it is a delicate matter and we would like to speak to the Bishop directly," Mario replied, trying to keep his manner polite.

"Please wait here," the man replied, then he shut the door leaving the two detectives waiting on the doorstep.

"Look on the bright side, at least it's not raining," Mario said to Pete as the door closed leaving them outside, exposed to the December elements.
"Fortunately, it's not too cold either," Pete commented, "but I find it a bit strange that they wouldn't allow us into the house while we waited."
"Meaning?" Mario asked succinctly.
"Meaning, it's not very Christian of them to leave us hanging around outside in the cold. I think they've got something to hide?" Pete replied as he cased out the front of the house, paying particular attention to the windows. He could have sworn he saw a curtain move slightly in one of the windows. But then his attention was drawn back to the noise of the door being unlatched and slowly opening.
"Good evening, my name is Bishop Denver, how can I help you?" The accent was East European and the Bishop was dressed in normal street clothes consisting of loafers, jeans and a golf shirt underneath a partially zipped up hoody. He looked to Mario to be in his fifties, but he was well-built, obviously kept himself in shape, so he could have been older. He was bald on top with a few grey hairs on both sides of his head that met at the back. He was clean-shaven, a kindly-looking face with small round glasses over his blue eyes.

"Bishop Denver? I hope you don't mind me saying so but isn't that an unusual name for a Serbian minister?" Mario asked with a smile, trying to break the ice.
"Yes, well, I discovered on my arrival in the United States that people were having difficulty saying my real name, so I legally changed it to Denver. The Broncos were playing on TV when I wrote out the application, hence Denver. But I'm sure you're not here to discuss the etymology of my name," the Bishop said.
"Of course not, Bishop," Mario replied before continuing. "We're investigating an accident that occurred at the circus on Sunday and we are looking for a Nikola Petrović who we think could assist us in our inquiries."
"And what makes you think I could help you?" Bishop Denver replied with a deadpan face.
"Petrović is Serbian and we were wondering if you were aware of any of his relatives or communities where we might be able to find him."
"I've never heard of a Nikola Petrović so I wouldn't know of any of his relatives. As for organizations, there are various Serbian communities scattered throughout the city, maybe you should contact them." The Bishop was rather terse with that last statement, Mario thought, and they still had not been invited into the house, which he would have thought would have been the polite thing to do. Obviously, Pete had been thinking the same thing.

“Bishop Denver,” Pete said, “do you mind if we come in, there are a number of potential scenarios we would like to run by you.” For the life of him, Mario could not think of a single scenario that Pete was conjuring up, but he clearly had a plan, so he would go along with it. But any hope of them entering the house was thwarted.

“I’m afraid not,” the Bishop replied abruptly. “You see, I’m hosting a small dinner party tonight and you are keeping me away from my guests. Now, if you’ll excuse me.”

Bishop Denver, without a simple goodbye or a by your leave, closed the door, leaving the two detectives on the doorstep looking at each other in total surprise.

“I think you’re right Pete, he’s hiding something,” Mario said.

“Or someone,” Pete replied. “I bet he has heard of Nikola Petrović?”

Friday 21st December 2018

Chapter 40

"Now, now," Humph said to Darlene as David left the room, "don't get yourself in a tizzy about him."

"But he and the other guy are so, so, arghhhh," Darlene said with clenched fists raised beside her head in rage.

"I know, but hey, let's not worry about him. We need to get me to the doctors and I don't want you driving mad," Humph said as he clumsily rose from his chair with the aid of his cane.

They made their way down to the underground car park in the building and lo and behold, they could see David in his car. The only light in the car was from his camera as he was reviewing the pictures, presumably the ones he had just taken of Darlene and the costume. Darlene was seething once more, and she was going to go over to him to give him a piece of her mind but Humph pre-empted her and grabbed her arm.

"Come on, now is not the time," Humph said and he dragged her over to his truck where he stood by the driver's side until she got in and put on her safety belt. Humph then moved around to the passenger's side and got in. They had taken to using Humph's truck as it was a state-of-the-art edition with all the bells and whistles. Compared to Darlene's beat-up old jalopy this was luxury and the decision had not been a difficult one to take during Humph's rehabilitation.

They arrived at Humph's doctor's office with a few minutes to spare for the appointment. Fortunately, the doctor's previous patient was just leaving the office, so they didn't have long to wait before Humph was summoned into the doctor's office by a nurse. Humph must have only been in the office about ten minutes before he came through the door beaming.

"Everything is good," Humph said enthusiastically. "I can gradually wean myself off the cane and I can start driving again! A case of win, win, win."

"That's great news Humph, now I can finally move back to my apartment," Darlene replied, rejoicing at the news. "So, let me get you home, pick up my car then I can go and begin sorting myself out for the holidays. I've done no shopping, no cooking, I have so much to do!" At those words, Humph was suddenly not so happy anymore, although he didn't reply to her until they were back in his truck and driving away from the doctor's office, with Darlene at the wheel.

"Look Darlene, I was under the impression that we had something going here," Humph began with quite some discomfort. "I mean why are you so eager to return to your apartment? I thought you were simply just going to stay with me!"

"Oh!" Was all that Darlene could muster in way of a reply. She had never been in a long-term relationship with anyone and although she had not considered taking care of Humph the last few weeks a chore, moving in with him had never entered her mind. Yes, their relationship had indeed gone to the next level but actually moving in to live with Humph had not occurred to her. She was forced to stop at a red light and she briefly looked across at Humph. He had that hang-dog expression, all pitiful and pathetic. She knew he thought the world of her, she didn't want to hurt his feelings but what to say?

"Look Humph, you've just sprung this on me in the middle of an investigation. What you're suggesting is a big step and it's happening too quickly. For now, I'll drop you off, get you settled in, pick up a few things, then I'll switch cars and go home to my apartment. I've got so much to do back there, let me sleep on it tonight, O.K.?"

Humph merely nodded, he felt that it was as diplomatic a way as any of dumping him.

Saturday 22nd December 2018

Chapter 41

At 7:30 AM the next morning, the whole team, with the exception of Humph, was in the office. This gave cause for concern for Darlene. It was not like Humph to not attend a meeting, especially knowing they were at a critical stage in the investigation. The team did some brainstorming but as far as any leads were concerned, regarding the whereabouts of Nikola Petrović, they were at their wit's end. It was looking more and more as if Mario was going to hand the case over to the authorities without getting close to their suspect. They were thrashing out a few possible scenarios on Darlene's evidence board when Harry walked into the office.

"Hey pretty boy, how's it hanging? Haven't seen you for a while," Harry said and walked over to Mario to give him a maternal hug.

"Nice to see you too. What are you doing here?" Mario asked.

"I'm working on a case with the Special Victims Unit. I thought I'd stop by here on the off chance you would be here so I could give you an update on the DNA analysis," Harry explained.

"Do you want a coffee Harry?" Darlene asked.

"No thanks, I won't be staying. It's just that it looks as if you were dead on about the costume switch," Harry began. "We haven't got down to the nitty-gritty of the actual DNA yet, but we know we have a plethora of different hair samples from that clown costume and I expect once we do the analysis, we will confirm your suspicions that they belong to Limpy and the Great Grando."

"Great that should provide proof of concept," Mario said unenthusiastically, which made Harry a little dejected as she thought her news would be received a little more reverently than it had.

"Darlene, did you give Harry the laundry bag?" Pete suddenly asked as he stood and looked over into the corner.

"Yes, I did," Darlene replied as she swatted away a small fly.

"Jeez Darlene, you've got a few flies flying around your desk. Where the hell did they all come from in the middle of December?"

"Well, if certain people had removed some dead flowers while I was working undercover on our last case then ***they wouldn't be here***," Darlene said shouting the last few words at Mario and Pete.

Pete merely smiled.

"Oh, don't be so hard on the flies Darlene. You must remember, if all the insects were to disappear from the earth, within 50 years all life on earth would end. If all human beings disappeared from the earth, within 50 years all forms of life would flourish."

"How do you know this shit?" Darlene asked.

"It was Jonas Salk who said that. The man who developed the polio vaccine," Pete replied. Before anyone could comment further, Harry's cell rang, she reached into her pocket to retrieve the phone and looked at the display, it was one of her team.

“Yes?” Harry asked. As Harry listened to the caller her face visibly changed to a mask of seriousness and worry. She turned to face Mario as she ended the call and returned her phone to her pocket.

“What’s wrong Harry?” Mario asked as all eyes were now on her as she began to speak.

“They’ve now isolated the DNA samples. They’ve confirmed that Limpy’s and the Great Grando’s DNA were indeed present on the costume but they have also found other hair samples on the helmet. They believe those to be from the Great Grando’s son.”

Saturday 22nd December 2018

Chapter 42

"I didn't even know he had a son!" Darlene said to no one in particular, as everyone else in the room looked just as perplexed.

"A third set of DNA? On the helmet but not the costume?" Mario asked, not believing what he was hearing.

"No, it appears there were only two sets of DNA found on the costume. One set belonging to Limpy and the other, the Great Grando, which is what we would have expected," Harry explained, "but to determine whose was whose, we needed something for comparison so we used the Great Grando's crash helmet and some used underpants from the laundry bag you gave to us."

"Oh gross," Darlene said as she squished up her face in disgust.

"That may be, but they are one of the best sources for accurate DNA samples," Harry explained.

"But wait a minute, since the accident, Nikola had been using that trailer, posing as Limpy. How do you know you didn't test using his underpants and not Limpy's?" Darlene questioned.

"You're right, that's a good question. The fact that it was Nikola who had been living in the trailer since the accident didn't occur to us when we selected the item for a sample, but fortunately, we now know that they are indeed Limpy's underpants and not Nikola's," Harry explained. "We took hair from Nikola's crash helmet that we'd retrieved on the day of the accident and compared them with those found on the costume. From the items we have now isolated three sets of DNA. First set, a match from the costume and the underpants, those belong to Limpy. The second set, from the costume and the helmet, both Nikola's. Third set from the helmet, Nikola's and his son, but who is that person? We can't tell you that, but based on the Y chromosomes they are definitely from a son of Nikola."

"But only Nikola used that helmet. Who else could leave their DNA all over it?" Darlene asked. A dumbfound look appeared on the faces of the investigative team and for almost a minute nothing was spoken. Then Pete's face lit up as all the tumblers fell into place in his mind.

"Anton," Pete said simply.

"Yes, but he was Nikola's assistant, there's a good chance he would have handled the helmet on many occasions," Darlene offered.

"Handling is one thing but there were numerous hair follicles found in the helmet," Harry explained. "He must have worn it for some length of time for that many to have been found."

"Oh no!" Mario suddenly blurted out and smacked the palm of his hand on his forehead. The full realization of what had happened during the explosion now came to him like a thunderbolt. "What if it was Anton that had climbed into the cannon and not Nikola Petrović."

"You got it," Pete said, smiling, knowing his boss had now twigged onto the plot. "If Anton is his son, that would also explain why he made such a hash of driving the cannon out of the arena. It was all part of the plan to destroy the evidence, which explains why both Anton and Nikola were on the scene so quickly after the fire. Anton was supposed to be in the vicinity of the cannon. It was his job to be there, so we didn't consider that a problem. He could have also helped Nikola move the body from the trailer to the cannon and place the body in the correct position for optimum destruction."

"Gwendoline had told me that they had both joined the circus within months of each other at a time when Petr, Nikola, the Great Grando, or whatever you want to name him, was asking for an assistant. What a coincidence? It's all beginning to make sense now. Nikola and Anton were both in on this together," Mario said.

"But it still doesn't explain why Nikola wasn't wearing the big blue shoes though," Pete said as he was trying to think this new theory through.

"Well, let's go back to our alternative theory on that," Mario offered. "Nikola knew there was going to be a hell of a fire, he didn't want to be traipsing about in something that would be a hindrance. He of all people would know the type of fire he would be dealing with! Chuck told us that the incendiaries would have done their job in the first few seconds. The rest of the fire was superfluous and the more they did to prevent jeopardizing the audience and to rescue the cannon the better."

"O.K., I'll buy that," Pete replied but everyone could see the cogs in his brain were looking for any flaws in the new theory. "But Humph had said there were no photographs of Limpy and the Great Grando together. If indeed it was Anton who got into the cannon, there should be some."

"Not necessarily, as we discussed yesterday, just before the fire, the performers were leaving the circus-ring so the chances of photos being available of the Great Grando and Limpy together would be minimal anyway. Furthermore, Nikola always knew that his plan could be sussed out, but he could still protect Anton if he gave the illusion that it was Nikola doing the switch and not his son. So as soon as the Great Grando was introduced and appeared in the arena, aka Anton, then Limpy, aka Nikola, retreated into the background," Mario conjected. "Remember, they were still trying to give the impression that it was suicide.

"Possible," Pete agreed, as he thought that one through. "When we first interviewed Anton, he was trying to push the idea that it was a suicide, knowing that we would eventually find the suicide note. I think you could be right Mario. Shit, now we must carry out an APB on a third person. They're going to love us."

"So much for our Christmas break, Darlene said.

"Wait!" Mario shouted and he held up his hands in a stop sign gesture, "before you do anything, let me get in touch with Gwendoline, she may know where Anton is. He may be resting on his laurels thinking he's gotten away with this." Mario dialed the number for Gwendoline's cell phone. She replied after two rings.

"Hi, miss me already?" Gwendoline answered, after reading the call display.

"Hey, not exactly. Look, we have a problem," Mario began. "Do you have any idea where we could find Anton?"

"Anton, why? What's he done now?" Gwendoline replied in a flirty sort of way as she teased Mario.

"I'll tell you when I see you but for now, I need to know where Anton is," Mario said with all seriousness, which got Gwendoline's attention.

"Well, I'm not his guardian, so I really have no idea," Gwendoline replied, pretending to be a bit miffed, "but I do know he is calling on me at my hotel room this afternoon. That was one of the things I had to do today, Anton has not been paid yet so he was meeting me to get his pay and expenses for his trip to Greensburg. He wasn't sure at what time he would meet me here, but he said sometime after 2:00."

"O.K., thanks for your help, that's all I needed to know," Mario said.

"That's it? Look Mario, what's this all about? Why are you suddenly so interested in Anton?" Gwendoline said in a hostile tone, she was not used to being bullied like this.

"Gwendoline, please, you have to trust me. I will explain when I see you. For now, don't let on to Anton that we had this conversation," Mario said, terminating the call.

"Right, Anton is arriving at Gwendoline's hotel at some point this afternoon," Mario said to the others.

"Are we going to apprehend him?" Darlene asked.

"No, we're going to tail him," Mario replied. "Perhaps Nikola needs money and Anton will be getting paid. Maybe Anton will lead us straight to Nikola Petrović!"

Saturday 22nd December 2018

Chapter 43

"We don't know the exact time Anton is going to show up. Gwendoline had said 2:00 but we need to be in position before he arrives, let's say 1:00," Mario suggested.

"There's three of us so we could have a forward tail a rear tail and a backup," Pete said.

"I agree," Mario said and then began giving instructions to Pete and Darlene. "Pete, you will be the forward tail. I'll keep fairly close to him a little behind him. He has never met me before so he shouldn't suspect that I am tailing him. Darlene, you can be Pete's backup but be careful, he's already met you so cover up your face."

"Are you expecting trouble with Anton?" Harry asked. "I mean, would he have actually been involved with either of the murders do you think?"

"We don't know for sure, but he may feel cornered if he knows we know that he was complicit in the cover-up," Mario replied. "He may lash out at the nearest person to him. That's why I don't want Gwendoline to know what we are doing. Right, I suggest we all be in position at noon." Darlene took a quick look at the clock.

"That probably gives me just enough time to swing by Humph's to see how he is doing and find out why he hasn't shown up here today," Darlene said. "I'll be there on time."

"Make sure your phone is charged and grab a radio for backup," Mario told her.

Darlene soon had her coat on and began leaving the office. "Take care," Harry called out to Darlene, as she walked past her. Darlene replied with a nod and a nervous smile.

"I'm starving, fancy an early lunch?" Pete said to the others.

"Sure, why not," Harry replied, before adding, "that young lady looks as though she's shaping up to be a good cop, but she seems a little concerned. Is she worried about her assignment?"

"It all depends on which assignment you are referring to!" Pete replied. "I think her assignment with Humph has hit a bump in the road!"

Saturday 22nd December 2018

Chapter 44

The previous evening, Humph had barely said goodbye to Darlene, he had been too devastated by Darlene's refusal to say anything. He had planned on the two of them having a steak and lobster dinner complete with champagne to celebrate his freedom to drive once more. Being a doctor himself, he had known the status of his injury and he was certain his physician was going to give him the all-clear, so he had arranged to have the necessary groceries placed in his refrigerator by his cleaning lady. Now instead, he sat in his armchair drinking a few glasses of scotch and eating his way through a big bag of potato chips. He knew Darlene would be freaking out if she was to see him eating those chips, but what did she care, he thought. The only reason she had bought them was for when he invited guests over during the holiday period. They were, as she had told him on more than one occasion, not for him. But Humph no longer cared. He certainly didn't relish the idea of cooking up a storm for one, so the chips would have to do.

After one more scotch than he should have had and once he had brushed the crumbs of an almost empty bag of chips off his shirt, Humph got up and staggered to bed. He undressed, leaving his clothes in a heap on the bedroom floor and just about fell into bed wearing only his underwear. The ringing of the doorbell woke Humph from a deep alcohol-induced sleep. It took him a while to orient himself and to realize it was now morning. The doorbell was ringing again and it was that noise that had woken him up. He struggled to get out of bed and staggered to the front door to see who it was. His head was killing him and every step was a momentous effort, and it had nothing to do with his bad ankle. With some difficulty Humph managed to squint one eye and look through the peephole in the door to see who was making all the noise, it was Darlene. 'Why didn't she just use her front door key?' Humph thought. Then it occurred to him that she didn't have one. All the time she had been staying with him she had been using his car-keys and the door key was on the fob. Slowly, Humph opened the door and as he did so he maneuvered his position so that Darlene couldn't see the state he was in.

Darlene walked straight in and as Humph closed the door behind her, she saw him in all his glory. She said nothing, but he did get the look.

Humph hobbled back to his bedroom to don some clothes while Darlene casually stepped into the living room to survey the remnants of Humph's previous evening's shenanigans. On the floor was an empty potato chips bag surrounded by crumbs, it gave the appearance that more of the snack had fallen on the floor than had gone into Humph's mouth. There was an empty, overturned scotch bottle on the side-table and another one that was half full beside it with the bottle cap on the floor. An expensive-looking glass crystal whiskey tumbler still contained some water. Darlene assumed it was remnants of the thawed ice that he had added to his drink. This had surprised her as looking at the mess, she wondered why he had even bothered making the effort to walk to the kitchen to get the ice. Then all was clarified as she saw the ice-bucket that belonged in the fridge. It was on its side, underneath the table. The contents of the bucket had melted long ago and had left a damp stain on the carpet. The television was still on. During his binge, Humph had tuned in to one of the cable channels that was showing old movies, but he hadn't really been watching them. Darlene searched for the controller, moving away discarded food wrappings until she had found it. She switched off the TV just as Humph came back into the room wearing sweatpants and a t-shirt.

"You look like shit!" Darlene said quietly and seriously as she looked at Humph. He was about to say something but stopped. He merely looked down at his feet like a schoolboy who had just been caught stealing from the cookie jar.

"Humph, you were doing so well on your diet, now at the first opportunity, you fall off the wagon. I'm really disappointed in you," Darlene said. Humph thought, nowhere near as much as he was, but he didn't think this was the right time to weigh in with that one.

"Look, something is up at the office. I have to go and meet the others but I just wanted to stop by to make sure you were O.K.," Darlene said and began to leave.

"Very considerate of you," Humph mumbled sarcastically. Darlene gave him another stern look.

"I have to go!" Darlene said and stormed towards the front door and out.

Saturday 22nd December 2018

Chapter 45

During the drive from Humph's to downtown, Darlene could not get Humph out of her mind and the thought of moving in with him. She was beginning to think that if his welfare concerned her this much then maybe she should, and he was certainly upset with her initial refusal. But as she approached the hotel Gwendoline was staying in, her mind returned to the case and she began to slow down. She spotted Mario along the sidewalk, idly looking into a shop window. Darlene managed to find a convenient parking spot on the opposite side of the road and she pulled into it. Before exiting her car, she donned a toque and a scarf, more for disguise than protection against the weather. Fortunately, it wasn't too cold for a December stake-out. She unplugged her phone from its charger and phoned Mario to inform him of her arrival and that she was just about to get into position. As Darlene stood on the sidewalk, she located Pete about two hundred yards away from the front of the hotel. From Pete's location he still maintained a line of sight with Mario.

It was shortly after 1:30 PM that Anton was first sighted and he was walking within yards of Darlene on the same side of the road. She immediately turned her back on him and began looking into the window of one of the many shops on the street. In the window's reflection, she saw Anton use one of the crosswalks to gain access to the other side of the street. Because Mario was unsure of who he was looking for, Darlene called him and provided a brief description of what Anton was wearing, even though his clothes were nondescript and like many of the other people crossing the road. Fortunately, Anton turned out to be the only person who made his way into the entrance of the hotel so it was easy for Mario to identify him. Mario signaled to Pete that their subject had arrived and Pete went on full alert, now it was just a matter of time before he left the hotel after meeting with Gwendoline. Anton would be forced to exit through the front entrance. Pete had checked with hotel security and discovered that because of the Christmas crowds all other exit doors of the hotel had been locked, except for emergency use.

At 2:05 PM, Mario's phone began to ring. It was Gwendoline informing him that Anton had left her room and he was now on his way out of the hotel. This was very considerate of her, Mario thought, as she had no idea that they were about to follow the unsuspecting Anton. Then, suddenly, it got Mario thinking, surely Gwendoline would have noticed it wasn't the real Limpy when he came to collect his pay. Then he recalled the answer to Pete's question when he had initially returned from holiday. Mario had asked, "do you have a suspect?" To which Pete replied, "Currently, I have two - Anton and your new girlfriend Gwendoline."

Saturday 22nd December 2018

Chapter 46

Mario tried to put the thought of Gwendoline being involved in the murders out of his mind, he was getting paranoid. There may have been an excellent reason why she hadn't noticed it wasn't the real Limpy. And yes, she was one of Pete's suspects at that time, but with all the evidence they now had at their disposal, there was no longer anything to implicate her, nor could he possibly see what motive she would have for being involved. Mario didn't have time to dwell on that possibility any longer because Anton had now come into view in the foyer of the hotel. Mario watched as Anton left the hotel, it was crunch time. If he decided to turn in the opposite direction from where Pete was waiting, Darlene would have to scoot ahead and cross the road to be the forward tail. Pete would then assume Darlene's position on the other side of the street. As expected, Anton turned in the direction where Pete was waiting. Pete was wearing dark glasses below a New York Yankees cap. He also had on a black winter puffer jacket and a neck gaiter that covered his mouth. Pete blended in with the many other New Yorkers doing their Christmas shopping. There was no way Anton would recognize him even if he got close to him. But even that eventuality was not going to happen as Pete began ambling along in the same direction that Anton was headed, maintaining his two hundred-yard lead. Mario tailed behind and Darlene was walking step for step with Anton on the other side of the street.

Anton was not sidetracked by any window shopping. He was focused on reaching his destination and the further they were walking along the avenue; the more Mario was convinced of what the destination would be. After about a fifteen-minute walk, Mario's suspicions were confirmed. Ahead of Anton, Mario could see that Pete was bent down, feigning tying up his shoelaces. He obviously had come to the same conclusion. It appeared to Mario and Darlene that if Anton kept walking in the same direction he was currently headed, he was going to have to sidestep Pete, but as he neared Pete, he turned, as Mario had expected. Anton began walking up the path towards the Parish House of St. Sava Cathedral.

Saturday 22nd December 2018

Chapter 47

Pete watched as Anton rang the bell at the Parish house. Mario began to increase his pace and he arrived at the corner where Anton had turned onto and stood beside Pete. Just in time to see Anton enter through the front door of the Parish House.

"Well, well, well," was all that Pete could say, as from his vantage point, he had seen Anton ring the same bell as they had done the previous evening. Except, that unlike them, Anton had been quickly admitted.

"I guess it's time for another visit to our friendly Bishop," Mario said. They both instinctively looked across the street to indicate to Darlene where they were going but she was running towards the nearest crosswalk to gain access to their side of the street.

The two detectives walked up to the door of the Parish House.

"You ring it this time," Mario said. "It didn't work for us last night when I did it."

"Ah, you think I have the magic touch," Pete replied as he rang the bell. There was an inordinately long wait and it didn't seem as if anyone was going to answer their ring.

"I'll bet you they're looking at their monitor and realizing it is us back again," Mario whispered. Pete rang the bell again, this time for a full five seconds as if he was sending them a signal that they were not going to leave until someone answered the door. Eventually, they heard movement inside and the door was slowly opened. The same flunky answered the door as had done the previous evening and he still had the same stern face.

“Yes, may I help you?” The flunky asked as if he had never seen the two men before.

“Yes, we would like to speak with Anton Depopoulis please,” Mario requested.

“I’m sorry we have no one of that name here,” the flunky replied, and he began to close the door.

“Let me put it another way,” Pete replied with his hand on the door preventing the flunky from closing it any further. “The man who just entered through this door less than a minute ago. We would like to speak to him, now. Alternatively, we’ll get a warrant to search the whole building and make sure that all these benefactors you have for the rebuilding of this church are aware that you are harboring criminals here!”

“One moment please,” the flunky said without even batting an eyelid as he gently closed the door. A few minutes later, the flunky opened the door once again, but on this occasion, they were invited into the house.

They were led through a hallway into a small living room cum office where they were asked to be seated. The civility was extended by offering them beverages but they both declined. After a minute or so of waiting it dawned on Pete that they were in a windowless room well away from the front door. It suddenly occurred to him that the delay in fetching the Bishop, offering them drinks, keeping them waiting, was all a deception. They were up to something.

"You wait here," Pete suddenly said to Mario as he rose from his chair. He then ran out of the room, retracing their steps back to the front of the house, just in time to see Bishop Denver about to close the front door. The Bishop was surprised to see that Pete had not remained in the room where his priest had taken them.

"What is it? What's wrong?" The Bishop asked attempting to both close the door while obstructing Pete from leaving the house, but Pete unceremoniously pushed the man aside and burst through the door.

Unaware that Pete had caught onto the Bishop's subterfuge so quickly, Anton had not used any great speed to depart the house and in a flash, Pete had grabbed the man's jacket and apprehended him. Pete was surprised that Anton had not put up any resistance. Anton merely stood there resignedly, allowing Pete to use plastic ties to secure his wrists and render him harmless. The Bishop had remained standing in the doorway with the door wide open. Pete used his radio to call Mario and he immediately came outside to see his partner standing there with Anton.

“I didn’t murder anyone. I had nothing to do with the killings,” Anton pleaded having recognized Pete.

“Maybe not, but you aided and abetted multiple murders. You knowingly withheld evidence, you lied to us, you tampered with evidence by driving over the crime scene. Each one of those is a felony. We’re going to throw the book at you sonny boy,” Pete told the distraught young man. Then Pete called in for a police cruiser to come and take Anton away.

“Please, it is not what it seems,” Bishop Denver said pleading with them. Mario looked at the Bishop, wondering what he could possibly mean but before any further clarification could be discussed, they heard a shot ring out from inside the Cathedral.

Saturday 22nd December 2018

Chapter 48

Darlene had finally managed to cross the busy road and ran into the approach to the Parish House where she had last seen Mario and Pete. She was surprised to find neither of them there. By now she was slightly out of breath, proof that she needed to get back to her regular exercises. Since looking after Humph her visits to the gym had dwindled down to zero. She needed to rectify that.

Based on last night's fiasco when talking to the Bishop she wouldn't have expected Mario and Pete to have been invited into the house so all she could assume was that they were searching the Cathedral. She looked around at the building that was enshrouded in tarpaulins and scaffolding together with signs proudly stating that the new roof will be completed by July 2019. There was also a brief account of the 2016 fire and the damage that it had caused. Today being a Saturday and with only a few days to Christmas, there were no workmen on site. Darlene returned down the driveway and walked the width of the front of the Cathedral, but she saw no sign of either Mario or Pete nor where they could have entered.

Darlene found a gap in the scaffolding and began walking along the front of the Cathedral to the entrance, a beautiful pointed archway that had been untouched by the fire, that led into the main building. The whole place was eerie, what little light that was penetrating the building from the outside cast ominous shadows and the infrastructure made creaking noises with even the slightest wisp of wind. She pulled a flashlight from the pocket of her coat, turned it on and began scanning from side to side letting the light penetrate the darkness of the interior. Treading carefully over rubble, beams and steel paneling that littered her path she was beginning to wonder why or even if Mario and Pete had ventured in here. Negotiating the obstructions, she began shining her flashlight in and around all the crooks and crannies of the Cathedral. To be on the safe side, she unholstered her gun and had it at the ready. She was beginning to think her being there alone was a bad idea and the fact that her backup team was nowhere to be seen was a good enough reason to begin retracing her tracks back out of the building.

Darlene began to turn when she heard a sound like someone tripping, followed by what could only be described as a blasphemous expression that was definitely not American. Darlene immediately spun back around.

"Halt police," Darlene shouted as with one arm she shone her flashlight and with her other arm pointed her gun towards the general sound of the intruder. She moved her arm in an arc in an attempt to shine the light onto who it was that was out there. That turned out to be a mistake because her action indicated to the intruder that she didn't know exactly where her quarry was located.

But that person could locate her because of the light from her flashlight. Darlene's initial thought was that the person who was out there must be Anton. Darlene assumed that he must have somehow eluded Mario and Pete and taken refuge in the rubble of the construction site. Unfortunately for her, it wasn't Anton who was hiding in the Cathedral, it was Nikola Petrović.

Saturday 22nd December 2018

Chapter 49

In his bid to escape the two detectives who had arrived for a second time at the Parish House Nikola Petrović had indeed tripped over some of the rubble-strewn around the Cathedral floor. During the detectives' previous night's visit, he had stolen a glance of them from his bedroom window. Nikola's initial thought was that, on this occasion, they may have returned with a search warrant, even though they had only asked to see Anton. In anticipation, stalling tactics were used to enable Nikola to escape through the adjoining hallway to the Cathedral and the Bishop helped Anton sneak through the front door. Using this diversionary tactic, the two detectives would be expected to chase Anton as he had been their intentional quarry. They didn't know for certain that Nikola was even there. This provided Nikola with the opportunity to escape undetected into the bowels of the Cathedral. It was thought that in the gloom of the Cathedral, amongst the rubble, finding anybody would be almost impossible. Nikola was expected to remain there, in hiding, until given the all-clear from the Bishop to return to the Parish House. But even then, he knew his days of remaining there in hiding were numbered and at some point, in the very near future, he was going to have to find alternate accommodation. It had been made abundantly clear to him by the Bishop that he had well overstayed his welcome. They could not risk harboring a fugitive any longer.

Right now, though, he had other problems. By the sound of the person's voice that had shouted out, he assumed it was that of a policewoman, probably the blonde detective who had been investigating the accident. The police had probably worked out what had happened at the circus and now here she was getting closer to where he was hiding. He reached gently into his jacket to slowly withdraw his pistol and then kept perfectly still. The light from the policewoman's flashlight was nearing ominously closer but it was positioned a little to his right so that when the flashlight arced it didn't quite reveal where he was hiding. He was concealed behind a pile of discarded rubbish, on top of which were two beams and he was looking through a small crack that was between them. Nikola had a good view of the approaching policewoman. She was in a crouched position as she slowly walked nearer to where he was hiding. The flashlight was in her left hand with the gun in her right hand. As the flashlight in her left hand scanned the area, her right hand followed in sync. Nikola waited patiently while she cautiously moved past his position then in a lightning-quick move, he was on his feet thrusting his gun firmly into the back of Darlene.

"Don't move a muscle or I will kill you where you stand," Nikola whispered menacingly through clenched teeth. Darlene knew it wasn't Anton's voice so she suspected it must be Nikola Petrović who was behind her.

"Killing a woman in the back shouldn't be a problem for you," Darlene gutsily replied, belying the fear that had suddenly welled up inside of her. Nikola ignored her comment and reached over to relieve Darlene of her weapon. He pocketed her gun and then took the flashlight away from her, switched it off and threw it to the ground. For a few seconds, all that could be heard was a slight wind in what was left of the Cathedral's rafters. Then suddenly Nikola pushed Darlene violently forward with such force that her feet hardly touched the ground as she traveled a few paces before tumbling to the dusty, floor in a heap of tangled legs and arms. Darlene laid there for a few seconds wondering if anything was broken then she slowly turned into a seated position on the cold stone floor. As she faced her protagonist, she could see the gun in his hand. It was fitted with a silencer, but what was even more scarier was the rampant evil in his face.

"So, you've figured out what really happened, have you?" Nikola hissed.

"We probably never would have. Limpy's murder could have easily been misstated as the Great Grando's suicide or death by misadventure. But you had to go and kill Shorty," Darlene replied. "That opened up the whole investigation."

"That was unfortunate. Shorty had entered Limpy's trailer totally unannounced," Nikola began to explain, "and there I was with all my greasepaint off and he saw who I really was. I had to kill him. Which upset all my plans. I was going to travel south, but not to Florida, I was heading to Phoenix. There is a large Serbian population there, I could easily get lost in Arizona. But Shorty messed it all up. I had to kill him and leave his body in Limpy's car. But of course, in doing so, I no longer had wheels, so I came here to the sanctuary of the church."

"Why would the church provide a murderer like you with sanctuary?" Darlene asked, buying some time as she tried to keep the conversation going.

"Oh, you'd be surprised how much influence I have and how I can, let me say, apply pressure to get what I want," Nikola said, boasting of his ability for extortion.

"Well, the gig's up Nikola. You're about to get what's coming to you," Darlene said, which of course was all a bluff, having no idea how she was going to turn the tables and get out of the predicament she was in.

"Ha, you and those other bozos you are with? I don't think so," Nikola chided. "Lady, you're very brave, I'll give you that, but I must not waste any more time. Stand up," and he gestured to Darlene to get up with an upward motion of his gun. Darlene slowly rose to her feet, testing for any breakages or sprains as she did so, while still watching as Nikola straightened his arm and pointing his gun directly at Darlene's head. It was then that she heard the sound of sirens for the first time, although it was a moot point anyway, she didn't think they were going to arrive on the scene in time to save her, but she felt she still needed to try and distract Nikola.

"By the way, why did you have to kill Limpy in the first place?" Darlene suddenly asked. It was the only thing she could think of to buy more time. She also really wanted to know the reason.

"Simple, he recognized me," Nikola said with a shrug of his shoulders. "He came to visit me in my trailer to formally introduce himself. We both knew of each other as performers, but our paths had never crossed. I guess from a distance I could have been anyone but once he was that close to me and listening to my accent, he knew instantly who I was. Pretending I was Macedonian would fool most people, but not necessarily those from that region. So, I was forced to kill him. Then I came up with the idea to convince everyone into thinking I had committed suicide by blowing myself up. The only difficulty was going to be how to get Limpy's body from my trailer to the cannon. That was when I brought Anton into the scheme."

"Your son!" Darlene said.

"Oh, so you've discovered that too, have you? Well done! Yes, Anton is my son. He assisted me in carrying the body into the cannon's area, then it was an easy task to move the body to the base of the cannon.

Then I had to become Limpy while Anton would become the Great Grando, well, at least for a day. So there, now you know. For all the good it will do you, as now you too must die."

Darlene was staring helplessly at the gun in Nikola's hand just as a cloud that had been obliterating the pale winter's sun, slowly dissipated. As Nikola stood on the stone floor of the roofless Cathedral, he became illuminated in beams of light, akin to a biblical figure about to perform a miracle. She could now clearly see the features of his face and the beginnings of a beard that she assumed would be part of his new disguise as he fled to Arizona. Darlene felt the scene was surreal until she was brought back to reality when Nikola took a step forward to obtain a better aim at her head. She heard his footsteps crunching on the debris under his feet as he came closer. The next thing she heard was a shot echoing around the cavernous edifice.

Saturday 22nd December 2018

Chapter 50

At the sound of Darlene closing the front door, Humph plonked himself down in his easy chair where all the dietary damage had taken place the previous night. Darlene had been right, of course, Humph thought. The first sign of a confrontation and he resorted to eating crap. That much drinking was not normal for him, but he really hadn't been thinking straight at the time. It was more of a case of whatever gets you through the night is what he had thought at the time. Now it appears he has also blown any hope of a long-term relationship with Darlene.

Then he snapped out of his post-drunken reverie and decided, regardless of what has happened, he needed to get back on track, with or without Darlene. He began clearing up his mess, wiping down the furniture and drying off the carpet. Once his living room was spotless, he attacked the kitchen and had it all spic and span he then turned to the bedroom, stripping off the sheets and placing them in the wash. He then made the bed with spare sheets from the closet before dusting and vacuuming the room. Once everything was up to snuff, it was time for a shower and a shave. By then he was feeling much better and decided to make himself a ham and cheese sandwich, garnished with lettuce and tomato, accompanied by a glass of water. He sat himself down in his favorite chair and once more turned on the TV and began scrolling through the oldies channels to see if there was a good classic available. He settled on an old western as he ate his lunch, being careful not to deposit any crumbs after he had gone to such great lengths to clean up the mess. Once he had finished his lunch, he carefully placed the plate on a side-table, then relaxed and watched the movie.

Despite sleeping in until late that morning he still managed to fall asleep and he was rudely awakened by the sound of his phone. Initially he thought it must be his mother calling, probably wanting to know which day he would be arriving for the Christmas holidays, but he was surprised to see the call display showing it was Mario.

"Humph here," Humph mumbled, still in a semi-comatose state from his sleep. "What's up?"

"Hey Humph, I was just checking that you were still at home," Mario said.

"Why? Where would you expect me to be?" Humph replied indignantly and uncharacteristically.

"Well you didn't show up at the office today. We were concerned about you," Mario said

"No need to be, I'm fine," Humph said.

"Look, we're on our way over to you right now," Mario said, with a hint of seriousness in his voice. "Just hang around until we get there, O.K.?"

"Hang around? What for? Why?" Humph asked, wondering why Mario should be telling him to stay at home.

"Humph," Mario said as his voice took on an even more serious tone, "I'm afraid there's been a shooting, we'll explain when we get there."

Saturday 22nd December 2018

Chapter 51

At the sound of the shot, Pete rushed into the Cathedral through one of the side doors, gun at the ready, while Mario remained guarding Anton. Mario called for additional backup and fortunately, there was a cruiser in the immediate area, and he didn't have to wait long until he heard the siren of a cruiser arriving.

Pete had entered the Cathedral, running in a crouched position. His eyes were still adjusting to the poor light when he heard another shot echo through the empty building and Pete stopped briefly behind a pillar before assessing the situation. In the gloom, Pete could see a figure and based on the man's height, he suspected it could be Nikola Petrović. His gun was being pointed at someone that based on the person's clothes, looked as though it could be a woman. Then the sudden realization hit him like a pile-driver. It looked suspiciously as if that woman could be Darlene, standing face-to-face with the murderer. But Pete's initial thought was what the hell was she doing inside the Cathedral?

Pete was about to shout out to the assailant when a number of events occurred all in quick succession. First, most of the Cathedral was suddenly illuminated by the builders' arc lights. Bishop Denver had also heard the shot and had followed Pete into the building. Knowing where the main switch was for the construction lights, having had to consult with the builders on a daily basis, the Bishop had wasted no time adding some divine light to the situation. The next surprising thing that happened was watching not only Nikola's legs crumple as his body fell to a lifeless heap onto the littered floor, but the person Pete thought was Darlene, also fell to the ground. Pete began sprinting towards the woman and the fallen gunman, but to Pete's big surprise, another man suddenly loomed out of the shadows. Pete had no idea who this person was but he could see that he was holding a gun. Pete stopped, went into a standard crouch position with both hands on his weapon as he pointed it directly at the stranger. Pete was about to shout out a warning to the new visitor, but the message would have been superfluous as the man raised his gun to his own head, shouted out a quick oath, and then fired.

Saturday 22nd December 2018

Chapter 52

Pete watched as the stranger fell to the floor and once he felt the situation was safe he ran over to the fallen woman only to have his worst fears realized; it was indeed Darlene. For the second time in the short period since the young female detective had joined the team, she had been placed in a life-threatening situation and as on the previous occasion, Pete was the first on the scene. Pete knelt down on one knee next to Darlene's prostrate body to assess her condition. Pete bent towards her to examine her for injuries, hoping for the best but expecting the worst. She was face down on the dusty, rubble-strewn floor and as he tried to examine her, he noticed her limbs were trying to slowly move, crablike over the dirt. Pete crouched down even further and gently touched her shoulder.

"Darlene, Darlene, are you O.K.?" Pete asked as softly as he could.

"You bet I fucking am," Darlene shouted unceremoniously. "He's got my gun in his pocket. I was trying to reach it until you came along."

"Well, I'm glad to hear you're fine," Pete laughed as a disheveled Darlene turned herself into a seated position and just looked across at Pete, who remained in his kneeling position.

"Where the fuck was you two? By the time I had crossed the road you were nowhere to be seen," Darlene asked indignantly. By now, Mario had joined them, and he answered the question.

“We didn’t know we were going to be invited into the Parish House,” Mario said. “Then Pete realized they were stalling us to give Anton and Nikola time to escape. Anyway, did you try contacting us?”

“Now you tell me! And no, I didn’t try contacting you,” Darlene said belligerently, realizing now that would have been the correct thing to do. Mario held out his hand to assist Darlene to her feet. Just then, Bishop Denver appeared and began providing last rites to Nikola who was lying face down with two bullet holes in his back.

“Tell me Darlene, if you haven’t been shot why did you fall to the ground?” Pete asked.

“What would you have done if shots were being fired and you couldn’t see where they were coming from?” Darlene asked Pete.

“Exactly what you did,” Pete replied.

“It’s funny what goes through your mind,” Darlene said, remaining surprisingly calm after the life-threatening ordeal she had just been through. “I heard the shot and my immediate thought was, ‘how did I hear that shot?’ It was so loud but Nikola had a silencer on the end of his weapon.” Mario looked down at Nikola’s piece to look at the silencer. “It took me a couple of seconds to realize it wasn’t him who had fired the shot and it wasn’t me that had been shot. That’s when I hit the deck.” Darlene took a couple of steps and reached into Nikola’s pocket to retrieve her gun, apologizing profusely to Bishop Denver for the interruption. Then she located her thrown flashlight that had lodged in the pile of rubbish that Nikola had been hiding behind.

"I guess he was too experienced to shoot you in here without the silencer. He would have known a shot would attract attention," Mario mused. "By the way, you seem to be in good shape for someone who has just faced a killer pointing a gun at you," Mario said, still gazing at the prostrate figure of Nikola's body. Meanwhile, satisfied that Darlene was fine, Pete had walked away to try and discover who the stranger was that had shot Nikola.

"Yes, but who's the other guy?" Darlene asked indicating with her head at the man Pete was now kneeling over, "he saved my life!"

"I have no idea," Mario replied as they both walked away from Nikola's body, leaving Bishop Denver as he went down on one bended knee to continue his ritual with Nikola.

As they approached the body of the stranger that killed Nikola, Pete began rummaging through the man's pockets searching for some id. but his efforts had revealed nothing.

"Any joy?" Mario asked.

"None, I have no idea who this fellow is and why he killed Nikola!" Pete replied. The three of them were looking down at the dead stranger when they heard the crunching of footsteps as someone else was walking slowly towards them. The arc lights didn't extend to the whole of the church and in the poor light, it was impossible to tell who was now approaching and whether they were armed or not so the three detectives instinctively drew their weapons and went into shooting positions. The noise of the footsteps was getting imperceptibly closer as the person loomed nearer.

Saturday 22nd December 2018

Chapter 53

"Don't shoot, please, don't shoot," the approaching person pleaded. As the person neared, Mario and Pete could now clearly see that it was Imam Marković holding up his arms indicating that he had no weapon. The three detectives relaxed their stance and put away their guns.

"Imam Marković, what are you doing here?" Mario asked suspiciously. After all, what was he doing in a Serbian Catholic church in the middle of what was now a crime scene? At the sound of the Imam's name, Bishop Denver looked up with a scowl at the intruder. The Bishop returned to completing the last rites on Nikola but now he appeared to continue with some urgency. The Imam looked slowly down with much sadness at the body lying at his feet.

"Inna Lillahi wa inna ilayhi raji'un," the Imam began, reciting a Muslim incantation for the dead man. "This is Darius, the man you wanted to interview before you discovered who the real killer was. I'm afraid I made the mistake of telling him the news you had given me yesterday evening and that you were coming here in search of that man." The Imam pointed over to the dead body of Nikola. "I received a call today from the couple Darius was staying with. They told me he went out last night and hadn't returned home. He must have thought that there was a good reason why you had come over here. I bet he stayed in this place all night, he must have arrived at the same conclusion you had and sensed there was a possibility Nikola Petrović was in the vicinity, but I have no idea where he managed to obtain a gun."

"Well, it was lucky for me that he did and was here when I entered the Cathedral," Darlene said.

The Bishop had now finished his incantations and began to storm over towards the Imam as if he was a trespasser, which in fact, it was exactly what he was. Mario decided to intervene.

"Bishop Denver, you told us that you didn't know Nikola Petrović, yet here he is," Mario said. You were harboring a fugitive, you lied to us. How do you explain that?" The Bishop came to a stop, he relaxed and took a deep breath before facing Mario.

"He threatened us. He told us he would only be here for a few days then he would disappear. He told us if we didn't hide him and keep quiet about it, he would blow up the rest of the Cathedral. He even threatened to harm members of my clergy. Are you aware of the problems we have had obtaining the money to restore this sacred building after the fire? We have had to sue the insurance company to pay out what we felt we were entitled to. Despite being in Manhattan our congregation is not a rich one. We have managed to get this far and I couldn't risk seeing it all come crashing down after the money that has been raised and all the good work that has been carried out, let alone the threats to my people." The Bishop explained, imploring forgiveness for not revealing Nikola Petrović's whereabouts. "And poor Anton, he was also a victim. His father was a tyrant, he had a kind of Svengali hold on the boy, as he did with many of us. Believe me, Anton is such a sweet boy he was forced to assist his father. What he told you is the truth, he took no part in the killings!"

After a short silence, the Imam was the first to speak.

"Detective, I have to leave; I will need to make the necessary arrangements for Darius's body to be removed." The Imam said. He was addressing his comment mainly to Mario but the Imam wanted to ensure the Bishop knew of his intentions, although he wouldn't look directly at him. He began to walk away, not even acknowledging the Bishop's presence.

"Imam Marković," the Bishop shouted out, "no need to leave yet. Please, come to the house and make your calls from there. We can help you contact whoever it is you need to speak to. Please come, too much death has occurred. We need to start healing, let us start right now and who better than us, to take that lead?" The Bishop was reaching out his arms, beckoning the Imam to return with him to the Parish House. The Imam had stopped in his tracks, but he had yet to turn around to see the Bishop offering his proverbial olive branch. Finally, the Imam slowly turned, he had tears rolling down his cheeks.

He didn't say anything, but he nodded his head and walked into the Bishop's outstretched arms. After a moment the two religious leaders broke their embrace and began negotiating the obstructions back to the Parish House, with their arms remaining around each other's shoulders. Other clergymen who had come out of the Parish House to witness the aftermath now began walking towards them and when they saw the two religious leaders together, they all placed their hands together in prayer. They mouthed silent prayers as they formed a gauntlet for the Imam and the Bishop.

"Don't we have to follow protocol and get Harry's team down here to process the scene before the bodies are removed?" Darlene asked as she was watching the entourage leave the Cathedral.

"I think we pretty much know what went down here Darlene," Pete said. "No police weapon was fired, so we don't have to involve our internal departments."

"It's just a straight murder-suicide case, witnessed by you and it will all be detailed in your report Darlene," Mario added.

"My report?" Darlene pointed to herself as she asked Mario with an incredulous expression on her face.

"Yes, your report, you were the one involved in this. We weren't even in the building," Mario said as he and Pete began laughing.

"But what about Nikola?" Darlene asked.

"Well, he can't write it," Pete quipped.

"Don't be ridiculous Pete. I mean, what about his body?" Darlene asked.

"We'll contact the organizations that need to know about the capture of war criminals," Mario explained. "We'll let them arrange to have his body removed from here and that will be that. After all, Commissioner Harper told me that it is outside our jurisdiction, right?"

"I don't think anyone is going to lose too much sleep over the murder of a wanted war criminal," Pete added.

"Not only that, we've solved our cannon crime, Shorty's murder and captured a wanted war criminal all in one afternoon. I think that's call for a celebration." Mario suggested.

"I just want to go home," Darlene said as her shoulders sagged and a wave of tiredness suddenly poured all over her.

"O.K., I can drive you home and Pete can follow behind in your car," Mario suggested. Darlene suddenly realized that after everything that had happened this afternoon, she didn't want to be left alone.

"Better yet, why don't you just drive me to Humph's."

Saturday 22nd December 2018

Chapter 54

Mario solicited a ride from one of the cruisers to return them to his vehicle that he had parked at Gwendoline's hotel. The three of them collapsed in the back of the cruiser and with sirens blaring they arrived in the car park in minutes. Mario thanked the officer for the ride and once they were out of the police car Darlene pulled her car keys out of her pocket and handed them to Pete.

"I'm parked just –," Darlene began to say but was gently stopped by Pete.

"S'O.K. Darlene, I saw you park, catch you later," Pete smiled and began walking to her car.

On the drive across the city to Humph's place, Mario called ahead to prepare Humph for Darlene's arrival. After the initial greetings, Mario got down to business.

"Humph, there's been a shooting, we'll explain when we get there!" Mario said with all seriousness. He expected to hear a concerned reply from the man, but he didn't expect to hear the subdued voice of someone who was obviously down in the dumps about something.

"A shooting? What are you calling me for?" Was Humph's indifferent reply.

"Because, I'm afraid it involved Darlene, and I thought you would want to know," Mario replied.

"What? Whaddaya mean shooting? Who? My God no, not Darlene!" Humph almost screamed as he began to fully realize the reason for the call. Mario smiled at Darlene and silently mouthed a cynical 'aaah' towards her before placing his phone on speaker and holding it between Darlene and himself so that she could also hear the conversation.

"Darlene was involved, but don't worry, she's safe. I'm driving her over to yours now. She wanted us to drop her off at your place." Mario replied, at that remark, there was a sound like a stifled sob before Humph answered.

"My place?" Humph managed to say as though he was totally surprised.

"Yes, your place. Why do you sound so surprised?" Mario asked and looked briefly across at Darlene.

"No, no, no I'm not, not at all. Why would I be? Right. But what happened?" Humph flustered out a reply.

"I'm sure Darlene will bring you up to speed when we get there. We won't be long now!" Mario said and then hung up the phone before again looking across at Darlene, "what's gone on between you two?" Mario asked.

"Just a misunderstanding, no biggie!" Darlene replied, staring out the windshield.

"Well, if it affects a member of my team or in this case two members of my team, then yeah, I think I might like to know," Mario told her, pretending to be an authoritative figure.

"Well, in that case, you're going to have to tell me what went on between you and Magill," Darlene replied with a wry smile.

"Touché," Mario replied and left it at that.

Mario pulled up outside Humph's house and Pete drove Darlene's car onto Humph's driveway.

"Will you be O.K. Darlene, or do you want us to come in with you?" Mario asked with some concern.

"No, I'll be fine, really," Darlene said.

"You did good tonight young lady," Mario offered as Darlene was unclicking her seatbelt, "but be bright and early in the office tomorrow. We have lots to do."

"I'll be there!" Darlene said as she got out of the car. As she walked up the driveway, Pete locked the car using the lock button on the key fob, then stood beside the vehicle holding her keys up by his side like some fancy hotel valet.

"See you tomorrow, kid," was all that Pete said as he smiled at her.

"Thanks, Pete," Darlene said with a tired smile as she walked up the gentle slope of Humph's driveway to the front door. Just as she reached the door it slowly opened and Humph stood there. He was now dressed in smart casual clothes as he stood in the doorway to greet her. Darlene turned around to wave to the others, by which time Pete had reached the passenger side of Mario's car and was getting in. Pete returned her wave, Mario waved too, and once Pete was in the car Mario took off. Darlene turned back to face Humph. Up until now, Darlene had not attempted to wipe off the dirt and grime that was mixed in with blood from a few lacerations that she had sustained during her encounter with Petrović in the Cathedral. She was desperate to take a long hot bath, but she also needed to tend to her wounds, although she was certain Humph would help her with that. She stood there in front of Humph as he looked her up and down. Her hair was plastered to her face, her disheveled clothes were a mess and she looked as though she was ready to drop.

"You look like shit!" Humph said. Darlene merely shook her head from side to side and then they both burst out laughing.

Saturday 22nd December 2018

Chapter 55

Mario and Pete returned to the office and during the next few hours and early into Sunday morning, they began communicating with the various police departments and agencies regarding the deaths of Nikola Petrović and Darius. Arrangements had to be made to retrieve the bodies which were coordinated by both Bishop Denver and Imam Marković. Of course, Mario's first call was to Commissioner Harper who had told Mario to leave it with him to call the appropriate authorities. But what the Commissioner really meant was to leave it to him to take the credit when he contacts the heads of the appropriate authorities who, in turn, will put the right people on to you to provide all the details for the grunt work.

Mario and Pete were expected to make an appearance at the Cathedral to explain exactly what had happened to the various representatives who had now descended on the crime scene. In attendance were representatives from the F.B.I., Interpol, CIA and a few state officials who were now surveying the bodies at the scene. After discussing the events leading up to the two deaths with Mario and Pete, all the agencies were content with the explanation, especially after it was collaborated by Bishop Denver and Imam Marković. Mario explained that the primary detective involved had suffered some injuries and was currently resting. That seemed to satisfy everyone, although, he was surprised at how little questioning was conducted by the authorities involved. Neither Mario nor Pete had ever been involved with war criminals before, so they hadn't known what to expect. On the drive to the Cathedral, Mario had thought he would be subjected to a thorough interrogation but in reality, it turned out to be more like a chat. It was almost as if the appropriate agencies were happy to remove the name of Nikola Petrović from their caseload. Once the body had been officially identified the authorities didn't seem to show any great interest in how the man's death had come about. Although they did request that a copy of the police report be sent to them when it became available, for their files.

Even though the death of Petrović was now official, it hadn't been announced publicly by any government department. On their return to the office, Pete called the young reporter that had supplied them with the digital photographs that had helped crack their case. He thought he would give him a heads up, despite the fact that the young whippersnapper had let the cat out of the bag when he had reported that the accident was, in reality, a murder. But, after all, he was a young kid just doing his job and Pete realized you never knew when you would need to call in a favor. Even though it was, by now, the early hours of the morning Pete knew the young reporter wouldn't mind. He was in search of the big scoop that would get him off the treadmill of reporting on community events and this could be it. Pete supplied him with sparse details, leaving out any reference to Anton. The information given was such that if the reporter would have dug deep enough, he could glean as much from other sources. Pete informed him there would be people at the Cathedral right now. Making a story out of it would be up to him.

By the time Mario and Pete had wrapped up all their loose ends it was just turning 5:00 AM. There was hardly any point going home. All the various interested parties were scheduled to appear in the office at around 8:00 AM and they were expected to remain there throughout the morning. So, Pete suggested a restaurant he knew nearby that would not only be open this early in the morning but also served the best English breakfast in the city. Well of course he did thought Mario.

Sunday 23rd December 2018

Chapter 56

Darlene and Humph laughed together because the *'you look like shit'* quote had been the last words Darlene had spoken to Humph when she saw him earlier that day while he was in that delicate state after his binge. Now, their appearances were reversed they had both seen the funny side of the situation. Darlene kicked her shoes off at the door then Humph began helping her navigate through the neat and tidy house to the bathroom. Physically, apart from the few scratches, she was fine, but the emotional affect on her was now beginning to take a toll and she needed the support of Humph's arm to keep her upright as they walked.

In the bathroom Humph immediately ensured the plug was in the drain then he turned on the water. Even though those actions took no time at all, Darlene now appeared distant, as if her mind was elsewhere. She had made no attempt to begin undressing so Humph gently extricated Darlene from her clothes, first her coat, then her top and bra. Humph undid the buckle of her belt, unbuttoned her jeans, and pushed them downwards to help them slide off her legs. She put her arms around his neck to provide balance as one leg at a time, she stepped out of the jeans that now laid in a heap on the terra cotta, tiled floor. Humph moved his hands to her hips and softly slid the tips of his fingers in between her waist and her panties. He was about to push down her underwear using his thumbs that were hooked over them when Darlene surprised him. Her arms were still around Humph's neck and with their faces so close together, she gave Humph a long, loving kiss. When their lips parted, Darlene returned to her almost comatose state as if the act had never happened. Humph resumed his doctor's persona and continued to undress her.

Humph asked Darlene to test the temperature of the water before he helped her into the bath. He knew she loved a hot bath but, being a 'shower' person, he wasn't sure as to exactly how hot she would like the water to be. She briefly tested the water with her foot while still hanging onto Humph for support and she then stepped into the bath, confirming the temperature was perfect. Once she stepped into the bath and sat in the spacious tub she closed her eyes, smiled, and lay perfectly still, letting the hot water soothe her aching limbs.

Humph gathered up her disrobed clothes and took them to the laundry room. He quickly returned to ensure Darlene's head was still above water.

"Can I get you anything else?" Humph asked quietly, trying not to impose on her serenity. Darlene almost imperceptibly shook her head.

"I could turn the jets on for you," Humph suggested. "I'm led to believe they're quite soothing."

"No, not right now. Thanks Humph, this is just fine," Darlene whispered. Humph left to retrieve some nice big towels and fetch her favorite pajamas from the bedroom. Contrary to what others in the department had been thinking, Darlene and Humph had been sleeping in separate bedrooms during his rehabilitation. Although their relationship had not been purely platonic and certainly close enough to possibly traverse to the next level, or so Humph had thought.

Humph returned to the bathroom and noticed Darlene had not moved. He placed the towels on a chair and hung the pajamas on the back of the door. Then he knelt down, picked up a sponge and began gently washing her. First, he washed her hands and arms, then her face, taking note of which scratches required further treatment. He used the detachable shower nozzle to wash her hair and was surprised to see how long it was as he had only ever seen it up in a bun for work purposes. Even outside the work environment, her hair was always up in some fashion. The wet strands now hung down to the top of her beautiful breasts, but then he was biased. In his eyes everything about her was beautiful.

When he had completed washing her, he helped her stand up and step out of the bath before drying her off. He sat her down on a vanity bench before applying antiseptic cream and dressings to the worst of the cuts. Once he had finished carrying out a quick physical, Humph then helped her into her pajamas. Supporting her they began walking slowly as they headed for her bedroom. The door of the bedroom Darlene had been using during her stay at Humph's was directly opposite his. Just as Humph turned to enter her bedroom, Darlene turned the other way and led him into Humph's bedroom.

Sunday 23rd December 2018

Chapter 57

The restaurant where Mario and Pete had eaten breakfast also prided themselves in their donuts. Mario came away with a couple of boxes each containing 12 of their finest, freshly baked donuts and he also arranged for an urn of coffee to be delivered to their office. By 9:00 AM, their office was the hottest spot in town. Word had carried like wildfire that not only was the cannon mystery solved but a war criminal captured to boot. Associates, like Chuck, wanted to stop by to extend their congratulations and representatives from both the F.B.I. and C.I.A. needed to obtain copies of evidence. The young reporter stopped by to personally thank Pete for the scoop. His name was Daryll Axesmith, and he promised to keep in touch and one day return the favor. Amidst all this clamor, a couple of the Commissioner's stooges walked in. They said nothing but took a quick look around and then left the office, which everyone thought a little strange. A minute later, the stooges returned, only this time led by the Commissioner himself. Apparently, as Pete explained to the others later, the stooges were sent ahead to ensure Limpy's costume and all clown-related memorabilia were no longer visible.

"Well, well, this is a cause for celebration!" The Commissioner stated. 'Kudos all around."

"Thank you, sir," Mario answered. "But I think most of the credit should go to Darlene who, once more, risked her life to apprehend the perpetrator." Mario indicated over to Darlene who was at her desk in the middle of writing her report.

"Indeed, well done Darling," the Commissioner replied. Then noticing some federal agents discussing photos with Humph, he decided his interests would be more beneficially served by talking to them. Darlene watched him go. Admittedly, she thought, I hadn't been in the department long but you'd think that by now he could at least get my name right.

Gwendoline had also stopped by and was sitting in the corner of the room by Darlene's desk, trying to remain inconspicuous. After a few moments of introductions and gushing hyperboles, the Commissioner suddenly noticed Gwendoline.

"Gwendoline my dear lady what are you doing here?" The Commissioner asked as he walked over to her and gave her a politically correct hug that could never be interpreted in any way as anything sexual.

"Oh, just here to support the team after all their great work," Gwendoline replied. "Mario and I hope to go out for a celebratory dinner this evening. I'm sure this steady stream of people will have stopped by then."

"Really," the Commissioner said, in a kind of surprised and jealous sort of way. "Yes, well I'm sure it will but I'm afraid police work never stops. No weekend breaks for us, hey Darling?" Darlene merely agreed by nodding her head with a smile and then rolled her eyes at Pete when the Commissioner wasn't looking.

"Just like working in a circus," Gwendoline replied, getting her digs in.

"Just like working here!" Darlene said under her breath as she continued typing into her computer.

"Well, I think you all deserve a break," the Commissioner declared, "Detective Simpson, once you've taken care of all these people why don't you and your team take some time off? Don't return to work until the New Year. You've been working on some high-pressure cases during the last few months. I'll see to it that your team will be excluded from any call-outs for the next little while. How does that sound?"

"Thank you, sir, much appreciated," Mario said although he was extremely surprised by the comment. He'd never heard of the Commissioner being so benevolent, but then there were some F.B.I. and C.I.A operatives within earshot. He was probably trying to look good.

"That means you can get an early start on the holidays. Well done everybody. Have a great holiday and a Happy New Year," the Commissioner shouted, being careful that his choice of words was not going to offend anyone in attendance practicing a religion that didn't celebrate Christmas. Then he left the office with his two toadies.

"Hey, that means you could all come and stay with me in Florida until the New Year," Gwendoline said.

"Sure where?" One of the F.B.I. agents jokingly replied.

"Not you, just this great team," Gwendoline chided the man.

"Ah, would love to, Humph replied. "Family commitments I'm afraid, but I'd gladly take a rain check."

"Not a problem, our first performance isn't until April, so you've got an open invitation until mid-March," Gwendoline explained. "Our winter site is just outside Sarasota, close to the beach."

"I may just take you up on that offer," Mario said, as the two of them began walking towards his office. "By the way, how do you know the Commissioner?"

"Oh, from various functions over the years, charities mainly. I really only know him as a casual acquaintance," Gwendoline said, then her face took on a serious tone. "Look, I really need to go, I have to start packing. I'm booked on an early flight tomorrow morning for Florida. You're going to be tied up here for the rest of the day, so I think I'll cut out now. Do you still want to make a night of it before I leave?"

"I'd love to," Mario said sincerely.

“Well, I’ll be in my hotel suite for the rest of the day, don’t be too late,” Gwendoline said seductively. She then began to return to the open area to say her goodbyes to the others, but Mario stopped her.

“Gwendoline, before you go, I need to ask you something,” Mario began a little tentatively. “Tell me, when the guy you thought was Limpy came to get paid and discuss his future plans with you, did you manage to get a good look at him?”

“I was sitting at my desk doing the finishing touches to my makeup for our dinner date when he knocked. He just said that he wanted to leave that night and that he would contact me in the New Year. I went to the safe to get his money. I put it in an envelope and handed it to him, that’s it.” Gwendoline explained with a quick hunch of her shoulders as if it was normal practice.

“But you must have seen his face?” Mario questioned.

“No, he was standing on the ground outside the trailer, reaching up over the half-door. We shook hands and he left,” Gwendoline said but then looked a little suspiciously at Mario, “why do you ask?”

“But there were a number of performers gathered around your trailer that evening, surely one of them must have seen the clown’s face close-up,” Mario said, ignoring her question.

“Maybe not. He had come up to the side of them and if he kept his back to them they may not have seen his face,” Gwendoline replied

but then thought of something, “maybe that was when Shorty first suspected it wasn’t the real Limpy!”
“Possible,” Mario thought and indeed that could well have been why Shorty followed Limpy to his trailer after he and Gwendoline had left for dinner. The good news was that Mario was quite happy to now dispense with Gwendoline as a person of interest in the case.

Gwendoline began to leave Mario’s office just as Harry came by and the two women exchanged pleasantries. Gwendoline returned to the open area to visit the rest of the staff and bade them farewell and looked forward to meeting them in Florida. When Harry walked into the open area with Gwendoline, Darlene noticed that Harry’s two photographers were not accompanying her. She saw this as her opportunity to have a word with Harry about the two guys’ conduct whenever Darlene was on the scene.

Sunday 23rd December 2018

Chapter 58

"Hi everyone," Harry shouted out and then gave a special smile to Darlene. "So, word has it that you were in the thick of things once again Darlene. You're making a habit of this."

"Just part of the job," Darlene replied casually before whispering, "Harry, may I have a word with you in private please?"

"Sure, what about?" Harry asked in a conspiratorial whisper.

"It's about your two photographers," Darlene said hesitantly. "I don't want to necessarily get them into trouble but..." Then her voice trailed away.

"Darlene, from my years of experience I feel if you want to talk to me about my staff, I would prefer to have Mario, your supervisor, present," Harry replied, still speaking quietly, but forcefully.

"It's a little sensitive," Darlene countered.

"All the more reason Darlene, sorry. If it was girl talk, or it's about working with these two dickheads," Harry tilted her head towards Mario and Pete in a joking gesture, "I would be more than happy to huddle, but if you're going to say something detrimental about members of my team then I would prefer to have Mario sit in so that there is no miscommunication or misunderstanding." Harry told Darlene.

Darlene was a little unsure about involving Mario. She hadn't been in the job very long and she knew that it would be a long time before sexual harassment would be completely eradicated from the workplace. But then again, she thought it never would be if people didn't speak up about it. Mario had now returned to the open area, having seen Gwendoline off, so Darlene took a deep breath and called Mario over.

"Mario, do you have a minute please?" Darlene asked. He was about to begin a conversation with Pete, but instead, he walked over to Darlene's desk.

"Sure, what's up?" Mario asked.

"It's about Harry's two photographers," Darlene began. "Every time we are on a case with them, I find them ogling and taking photographs of me. You can also ask Humph and Pete. They've witnessed their stares. Look, I'm not a prude, I'm a big girl. I've been through this before. I can take most of the crap, but it came to a head the other night when David arrived to pick up the clown costume. His behavior was so blatantly obvious. He asked me to stand first on one side of the costume, then on the other. He wanted me in all the shots. He claimed it was to obtain size perspective, but I think he was just trying to take photographs of both sides of me. I find it degrading and it makes me feel very uncomfortable."

She expected that there would be a reaction from Harry, defending her staff, but what she got was totally unexpected.

“He ***was*** trying to get photographs of both sides of you!” Harry replied and burst out laughing.

Sunday 23rd December 2018

Chapter 59

Harry's outburst had caught the attention of Humph and Pete, so they ambled over. But now Darlene was miffed. She was expecting a little more empathy from Harry.

"Sorry Darlene, I don't mean to belittle your concern, but you couldn't be further from the truth," Harry told her, struggling to speak during her laughter.

"What do you mean?" Darlene asked. "Their looks were real."

"Sure they were!" Harry replied as she began to get control of herself, "but both guys are happily married, and as beautiful as you are Darlene, they're just not interested in you as a sexual object."

"Being married doesn't make a difference," Darlene countered.

"No, it doesn't but you don't understand," Harry suddenly looked pensive before she continued. "I'm sorry, maybe I should have mentioned something to you sooner. Let me explain, you have to remember all young police photographers are wannabee fashion photographers. When Dave and Mikey first saw you, they were not struck by you, per se. It was your symmetry."

"My what!" Darlene said.

"Your symmetry. What the guys told me, and believe me, they told me that the first time they met you. They explained everyone has a preferable profile, that's the side all celebrities would prefer to have taken of them during photo shoots. It is very rare that someone, like yourself, has an almost identical symmetry where you don't have one side better than the other. In their opinion, both your profiles are equally as good as one another. They were fascinated by this," Harry elaborated.

"Twiggy." Pete said.

"What?" Darlene asked.

"Not what, who. Twiggy," Pete repeated, "she was one of the top fashion models during the swinging sixties in London. Apparently, she was in so much demand mainly because of what Harry just said. During a fashion shoot, the photographers could just keep clicking away without caring which side of her face was being taken."

"Exactly," Harry said, "so no, they're not trying to get into your pants. Their interest is purely professional, it's a compliment Darlene, really it is. Nevertheless, I will tell them to back off or at least, in the future, get them to always ask your permission before they start taking photographs of you."

"Talking of pants, it reminds me about the samples you used for DNA testing," Pete said. At first, the others thought he was going to raise an important issue, then they all groaned knowing what was coming.

"Yeah, an old couple went to the doctor. After a thorough exam of the gentleman, the doctor said, "I'm going to need samples of your blood, urine, feces and semen." The old guy, being a bit deaf, asked his wife, "what did he say?" She replied, "give him your underpants!"

Sunday 23rd December 2018

Chapter 60

"On that note, I think I'll take my leave. I'm still working on that Special Victims case," Harry said before putting a hand gently on Darlene's shoulder and looking her directly in the eyes, "are we good?"

"Yes thanks," Darlene said, placing her hand on Harry's to endorse what she felt.

"Don't be too hard on the boys, Darlene, they're really nice guys," Harry said quietly to Darlene before turning back to the others. "Have a great holiday guys and, see you all next year," she then waved to everyone and left the office.

"How much longer do you think you'll need to get that report finished, Darlene?" Mario asked.

"Another couple of hours I guess," Darlene replied.

"Good timing for lunch," Pete responded.

"Great idea, my treat," Mario said, "that will give Pete and I time to finish documenting Anton's interrogation, then I can distribute all the paperwork and we're done."

"Oh, by the way, what did you learn from Anton's interrogation?" Darlene asked.

“He pretty much confirmed what we suspected,” Mario replied. “The switcheroo in the cannon, as Harper calls it, was exactly as Humph had suggested.”

“What about detonating the explosives? How was that done if he had climbed out of the cannon?” Darlene asked.

“During normal performances, there’s a switch inside the bore of the cannon that is used to activate the firing of the cannon,” Pete explained. “This switch is also hooked up to a detonator that triggers the fireworks. But there is also an auxiliary switch at the base of the cannon that could be activated for running tests using dummies to check weight options. During testing, the trigger for the fireworks can be deactivated. Of course, during the fatal performance, it wasn’t. On the day in question, after removing his Great Grando tunic, Anton climbed out of the cannon and pressed the auxiliary switch. The tension of the spring on the cannon was set to just enough pressure to push the fiery body of Ahmed to the lip of the bore where gravity did the rest and it fell to the ground.”

“As you told me at the beginning of all this, simple when you know how!” Darlene said looking at Pete. “But surely Anton would have been sweating profusely after wearing his clothes under the costume and the exertion of getting in and out of the cannon.”

"I'm sure he was, but who would have noticed him with the fire blazing away and everyone helping to try and put it out?" Pete asked. "Everyone would have been sweating bullets by then."

"True," Darlene acknowledged.

"As for the rest of the story, we pretty much knew what had happened. Both Limpy and Shorty had recognized Petrović, so they had to be eliminated. In Shorty's case, simply wrong place, wrong time," Mario explained before continuing, "but it looks like Bishop Denver was right, Petrović had a hold on Anton. Petrović arranged for Anton to come to America as soon as he got the gig with the circus. Petrović had got the gig by lying to Gwendoline about his past experience in the circus in Europe. He provided references that consisted of real names in defunct circuses. The contact information looked legit, and when she called the provided numbers his experience was confirmed. He had that much pull back in his home country that he could arrange all that, even to the point of receiving training as a human cannonball. It was like an underground witness protection service."

"But how did he persuade Anton to join him and get involved in all these criminal activities?" Darlene asked.

"Well, Anton's mother still lives in Serbia," Mario continued. "Turns out that Petrović's tentacles still stretch back to some criminal cohorts in the old country. He needed Anton over here to run errands and carry out underhanded activities. It appears that Anton was forced to carry out Petrović's bidding or his mother would have been harmed."

“But when we initially interviewed Anton he seemed so genuinely distraught as if it really was his mentor that had died,” Darlene said.

“I think it was because he was upset at the web of deceit he was involved in. He wanted to confess, but he couldn't,” Mario suggested.

“Poor guy, so is his mother still in danger?” Darlene asked.

“The authorities are trying to locate the mother as we speak and when they find her, they will bring her stateside for her own safety,” Mario replied. “Consequently, we will complete our reports, they will all be considered confidential and we will pass them onto the appropriate authorities. We will have no further part to play in the proceedings.”

“So, Anton will not be charged with anything?” Darlene asked. She had been taken totally by surprise by what she had just been told.

“Apparently not, he is being considered a victim in all of this,” Mario replied.

“Man, he really fooled me with those crocodile tears when we first interviewed him, trying to convince us it was a suicide. Which begs the question, why aren't they going to press charges against him? There's obstruction of justice, I mean, he lied to us, then there's aiding and abetting?” Darlene asked.

"They will almost certainly all be dropped. After all, what crime did he commit, really?" Pete asked, rhetorically. "It's not as though he committed the murders himself. He wasn't even present for either of them and any assistance that was given to Petrović to dispose of the bodies and the destroying of evidence was under duress."

"But the lies he told us. It could have saved us a lot of time and trouble if he had simply told us the truth," Darlene replied.

"True, but put yourself in his shoes. I'm sure you would have been just as mendacious? We could even say the same about the Bishop and the Imam, of all people. They both lied to us too!" Pete said.

"What a veritable farrago of lies and truths!" Humph said.

"Farrago?" Darlene silently mouthed toward Pete, her face creased in confusion.

"Hodgepodge," Pete replied in kind.

"So, what's going to happen to Anton?" Humph asked.

"They're going to keep him in a safe house and question him further regarding his father's activities. He may be able to help with some suspicious contacts both here and in Europe. Once his mother is rescued and brought here, then they're probably going to put them both in the witness protection program," Mario explained. "You never know, he may be seen being fired from a cannon sometime in the future."

"Would Gwendoline take him back on?" Darlene asked.

"Who knows? That's entirely up to her, but for now, we can't even mention it to her. All very hush-hush you know," Mario stressed.

Over lunch, courtesy of Commissioner Harper they all discussed their Christmas plans. Pete would be spending Christmas day at home with his wife and children. They would be joined by his brother's family for breakfast and his in-laws for dinner, together with his mother. Mario would be staying at his parents' house beginning Christmas Eve and not returning to his own apartment until two days later, stuffed and happy. Humph would be staying in Boston with his parents. They usually have a big family reunion with the rest of the Lazenby clan. That left Darlene who said she would be visiting her home in Harriman, where she had spent every Christmas for her entire life. Humph was a little disappointed, he had been hoping to spend the holidays with Darlene. Although he certainly understood why she would want to spend the holiday with her mother, recalling the visit he had made with Darlene to her family home during their last case and that almost endless supply of delicious homecooked goodies. He could only imagine what Christmas dinner would be like in that household. Then a quirk in Darlene's logic suddenly hit him like a thunderbolt.

"Wait a minute, isn't your mother still on a cruise with old Chief Horowitz?" Humph asked.

"Yes, but I'll still be at home. My mother has probably already cooked up a storm and left it all in the freezer," Darlene replied, albeit a little sadly. "Anyway, it's my tradition."

"Having had first-hand experience of your mother's cooking prowess, I'm sure you won't go hungry, but you will be all by yourself Darlene!" Humph remarked.

"Hey, it's not just my mother who can cook in my family. I can cook too you know!" Darlene replied indignantly.

"Yes, I can certainly attest to that, Darlene, but Christmas alone? No, that won't do, young lady," Humph replied emphatically. "This year you will be spending Christmas at the Lazenbys' homestead. You will be starting a new tradition. We leave tomorrow!"

"Humph, I couldn't possibly," Darlene began to say.

"Tut tut tut tut," Humph replied as he wagged his finger at her in a '*no you are not*' gesture, "it is not open to negotiation. You are coming with me and that's that," Humph said forcefully.

"Ooooh, I'm not so sure about that. A commoner accompanying Humph to the Lazenby mansion!" Mario teased. "A mere policewoman amongst all those doctors and lawyers."

"Away with you Mario. My parents have already met Darlene a couple of times and they love her," Humph shot back. "They came to visit me at my home to make sure I was being well looked after and they were more than satisfied I can tell you."

"And the rest of Humph's family will be sure to love you, Darlene. After all, you have perfect symmetry!" Pete joked.

"That reminds me, while we're back on the subject of that. Pete, how did you know that shit about the celebrity, what was her name again, Twiggy?" Mario asked.

"Oh, the model. Well, apparently my mother idolized her back in the day. It wasn't so much for her looks, although she was attractive, still is actually, but more because of all the latest mod clothes she was always seen in. She was a trend-setter," Pete explained.

"No, that's not the real reason," Darlene said, looking directly at Pete. "The truth is you have hyperthymesia." The others stared at her as though she was an alien that had just been beamed to the table.

"What the hell does that mean?" Pete asked.

"It's a condition that enables individuals to be able to remember an abnormally large amount of information about their life!" Darlene explained proudly, believing it summed up Pete to a tee. Although it did fit the bill, the real reason was that Darlene was getting even with Pete for once and she beamed at him with a mischievous smile. To which Pete replied.

"How do you know this shit, Darlene?" They all laughed!

ACKNOWLEDGEMENTS

The author wishes to thank the following for their technical expertise:

Terry Connolly for his thoughts, insights and critiques.

Claire Stavros for her support and assistance.

Cindy Leich for her exhaustive proof-reading.

Needless to say, any errors or omissions in this novel regarding the areas of expertise remain the fault of the author.

<u>AVAILABLE SOON:</u>

Murder of a Valentine (another Mario Simpson mystery)

Genesis Déjà vu – The Early Years (the third book in the series)

To join the mailing list, email:

DEXTER-JAMES@OUTLOOK.COM

Manufactured by Amazon.ca
Bolton, ON

19062928R00144